Margaret Bottome

A Sunshine Trip

Glimpses of the Orient

Margaret Bottome

A Sunshine Trip
Glimpses of the Orient

ISBN/EAN: 9783337258832

Printed in Europe, USA, Canada, Australia, Japan

Cover: Foto ©Andreas Hilbeck / pixelio.de

More available books at **www.hansebooks.com**

A Sunshine Trip

GLIMPSES OF THE ORIENT

Extracts from Letters

WRITTEN BY

MARGARET BOTTOME

EDWARD ARNOLD

NEW YORK   LONDON
70 FIFTH AVENUE   37 BEDFORD STREET

1897

University Press:

JOHN WILSON AND SON, CAMBRIDGE, U.S.A.

TO

MRS. NORMAN L. MUNRO,

WHO MADE "THE SUNSHINE TRIP" A POSSIBILITY,

This Little Volume

IS AFFECTIONATELY DEDICATED.

Contents

Contents

INTRODUCTION.

LIFE is too short to permit one to refuse to do anything in one's power to give pleasure to others. Acting on this principle, I consent to let this very imperfect account of my trip to the East go to those who insist on having it. I have been waiting for the time to come when I should have leisure to write more at length; but alas! that time has not yet arrived. The best I can do is to give these extracts of letters I sent from the East, imperfect as they are. If in this way I can give pleasure to any one, I shall feel amply repaid.

M. B.

A Sunshine Trip

ON THE OCEAN

BLUE skies, smooth seas; all the glories of sunrising and sunsetting; the Atlantic Ocean so beautiful that it seems no longer the "unpastured sea hungry for calm!" It appears as if it had entered into rest.

These days and nights we are spending on the "Fuerst Bismarck"; the new friends we are making; the beautiful sights we see on this ocean, day after day! Really, it does seem to me that never till all earth's beauties disappear, and we come in sight of the New Jerusalem, and sit down together by the side of "the pure river of water of life," shall we have anything so perfect as our voyage to the lands that will be new to most of us.

It has been the dream of my friend's life to see the Holy Land. I am sure I never dreamed I should see it; but my friend's dream has made it possible for me. What a happy party we are! Since the morning of January 28 (the most beautiful winter day I ever saw) we have had the same blue skies and smooth seas; and, if this continues, I think our trip could most appropriately be called a "Sunshine Trip."

I need not describe ship life to you who know it; and yet this is so different from the ordinary voyage across the Atlantic! It is a Southern trip in more ways than one. Acquaintanceship soon ripens into friendship, for you must remember that we are living together for a

long time. When we go into the din-
ing-room we look on the right for our St.
Louis friends as if they were our guests
or we were theirs.

Of course it is always Egypt and the
Holy Land with us; and yet we enjoy
everything on the way. I mean, as best
I can, to let you know at least a little of
each place at which we shall stop on our
way to Alexandria, and if you get only
a few lines from a place you have never
visited, it may be of interest to you.

I am delighted that we are to stop at
so many places that will be new to me.
I think we are all prepared to act on the
suggestion of Archbishop Trench, —

> "Wise it were to welcome whate'er of joy, though
> small, the present brings :
> Kind greetings, sunshine, songs of birds and flowers,
> with a child's pure delight in little things.
> And of the unborn future rest secure,
> Knowing that mercy ever will endure."

ALL here is new to us, — new people,
a new mode of travelling, and a
climate that almost makes you feel you
have reached the land where everlasting
spring abides. We are told the island
was discovered by an eloping couple,
who, fleeing from Portugal to France on
a small vessel which was blown hither
by adverse winds, were left by the crew
of the craft. They lived and died here,
and the oldest church in the place is built
over their graves.

It seems to me that the spirit of love
still broods over the place. I shall
always remember it as the place where
white roses were thrown into the window
while we were ascending the hill in a
little open railway-car, with the tropical

gardens on either side of us. The flowers which are considered rare by us are the common flowers here. For a moment I caught a sight of what I imagine Paradise will be. It almost seemed as if the "loved of long ago" would come to meet us with white flowers. And in the little church on the top of the mountains, called "Our Lady of the Mountains," so profusely decorated with the beautiful japonicas, it seemed as if all church distinctions vanished, and we all felt like kneeling and returning thanks for the beautiful voyage we had had over such a lovely sea.

In that little church I saw a sight strange to me. On the wall I noticed a leg made of plaster; a little distance from that, a hand; and, not far off, a foot. Not long after, while talking to Father McL—— (whom we all en-

joyed so much on the " Bismarck "),
I asked him what it signified. He had
not noticed it, but he said, " Undoubtedly
some one has suffered much, and perhaps
has had a limb amputated, and, his life
being spared, to commemorate the mercy,
has had a plaster cast made of the limb
and hung it in the chapel." " Well,"
I said, " I am glad you told me. There
are many people who ought to remember the great mercies of their lives and
yet have n't had so much gratitude as
these poor people." The word was
not slow in coming to my mind, " I
beseech you, by the mercies of God, that
ye present your bodies a living sacrifice." The feet that have been spared,
the hands that are still ours, — shall we
not dedicate these living feet and arms
to the service of the One who made them
and has preserved them for us?

HERE I am at Gibraltar! This rock has had a peculiar fascination for me from childhood, though I never expected to see it. How often I had heard my mother say, "You could not move her any more than you could move the Rock of Gibraltar." You will remember that the rock was known to the Phœnicians as one of the Pillars of Hercules, the point on the opposite African coast being the other pillar. West of these pillars, which were named for the deity, and not the hero, the ancients supposed there existed nothing but darkness and chaos.

I stood and looked off on the two con-

tinents, and had one of my usual reflections. How little those ancients dreamed
of the beyond ! They thought they had
it all. How little did they dream of the
Western world ! Standing on a spot
where the African coast was so near, I
thought of the great Beyond, not bounded
by our North and South, and East and
West. I left the spot, murmuring the
lines of Whittier's, —

> " I better know than all
> How little I have gained,
> How vast the unattained."

It was interesting to go through the
galleries which honeycomb the rock ; and
looking through the little openings out
on the beautiful sea makes you think
of the pleasant things that come to you
while passing a rocky way in life, where
you get for a moment a view that tells
you it will not always be a rock. I need

hardly tell you that I saw a lesson in the fact that a variety of plants and trees and shrubs flourish among the stony ledges and crevices.

Around the point we saw the summer residence of the Governor. Beyond that an inaccessible cliff rises in a perpendicular wall of rock from the sea. For the first time I stood on Spanish soil and saw the contrast between a British and a Spanish town, and I could not but feel as if I would like to have England own everything on the footstool, excepting, of course, the United States. Say what we may about the British Lion putting its paw on everything, I notice that where that paw is, there is civilisation.

We were in Spain for a few moments only (and were glad hurriedly to leave), and saw only the wretched little town of Lima, where the bull fights are given on Sun-

days and fête days. The utter wretchedness of the place, the extreme poverty
and filth, made us say, " Take us back to
British possessions." The Spanish may
dream that the rock is only temporarily
under the British flag ; but no one who
steps on Spanish soil, it seems to me, and
then goes back to where the British flag
floats, will fail to say, " Long may it
wave."

IN 1830 the French took possession of
this city, and have held it ever since.
It was intended, I have heard, that Algiers
should be restored to the sovereignty of
the Sultan of Turkey, but Louis Philippe
decided to retain the conquest. I am
glad that the Sultan does not own it. I
seem now to see the dazzling white houses
as they looked to me, with the early sunlight on them, that beautiful morning
when we came in sight of them. The
houses rise from the water front with such
regularity and in such a mass of greenery
that I do not wonder the natives say
Algiers is a diamond enclosed in an em-
erald. Here we first caught sight of what,

we are told, we shall see along the entire coast. The Arabs bring their Oriental goods to the steamer, and on the morning I speak of, our deck was transformed into a fascinating shop. All kinds of curious things are offered for sale, not only Egyptian, but Moorish; and the prices are not unreasonable. We were told to wait till we reached Cairo before making purchases. We spent Sunday here. Of course we wanted to go to service, so we took a carriage, asking to be driven to the English Church; but the driver stopped at the mosque "El Tebir," built in the tenth century, and a fine example of Moorish architecture. Our courier said we had plenty of time to see this mosque: so here we had our first experience in putting on the usual slippers, for we could enter the mosque only with sandalled feet.

We shall not get so many opportunities

of going to church on this trip that we shall be apt to forget the sermon in that English Church, or the service that never seemed sweeter, or the hymn that was more to me than all I had heard since leaving New York, — " I could not do without Thee." How often Mrs. M—— and I have repeated the words, " I could not do without Thee " ! So just now, instead of telling you of more of the outward, let me repeat, as the beautiful Algiers is fading from our sight, the words of the hymn, sweeter than ever before, sung in that little English Church : —

> " I could not do without Thee, —
>   No other friend can read
> The spirit's strange, deep longings,
>   Interpreting its need.
>
> No human heart could enter
>   Each dim recess of mine,
> And soothe and hush and calm it,
>   O Blessed Lord, but Thine."

Ah, me! I wish that the poor Mohammedans that we saw prostrate themselves
in their mosque that Sunday morning
only knew the true Prophet and King, —
our Lord Jesus Christ.

How shall I describe that lovely Sunday afternoon after our dinner at the
hotel? As we walked through the avenues,
with their hedges of cactus and roses on
every side, everything seemed so strangely
beautiful. At last I saw palm trees large
enough to satisfy me. I smiled at rubber
trees huge as maples or oaks, and thought
of the little miniature rubber tree I had
left behind me at home; and I said to
myself, when I see it again I will tell it of
its grand relations in Africa; for it is a
comfort to know you are respectably connected, though you may never see your
rich relatives. Algiers will always have a
fascination for me.

Algiers

On Monday afternoon we were all
on board our steamer and were sailing
for the South of France. How home-
like the steamer has become to us; how
pleasant the greetings with one another,
after a day on shore, — the telling each
other of our impressions and showing
purchases made; all so companionable
that it is no wonder the very name of the
" Fuerst Bismarck " will ever have a pleasant sound for all of us !

WE arrived at Nice on the morning of the twelfth of February. The fairy scene continued, the weather being perfect. As we stood at the station waiting for our train, we saw an empty railway carriage, and, thinking it was our train, we hastened to fill the empty seats. When all were nicely seated, up came our guide and said, " Will you please get out." Of course, there was nothing to do but get out ; and then he said in his imperfect English, "Please see that I am in front of you, and not behind, in the future." I need not tell you I thought of the times when I had gone ahead of my Guide.

Villefranche, Monte Carlo, etc.

The familiar lines came back, —

"I would be treated as a child
And guided where I go."

"Follow your guide." If that train had moved, we should have gone exactly the way we did not want to go, —the wrong way. Alas for the many who have taken the wrong train in life !

Our visit at Nice was most agreeable. The climate, as elsewhere, is absolutely perfect. But the object of painful interest was Monte Carlo, famous for its great gambling establishment. Our visit to Monte Carlo was in the evening. In order to obtain entrance to the gambling-rooms all are required to give their names and addresses. It was the first and last time my name will stand as a visitor to the gambling hell at Monte Carlo or any other such place. The grounds are en-

2   17

trancing. They are filled with immense varieties of trees and shrubbery, and at last I saw every variety of the palm family of which I am so fond. Ascending the marble terraces, you get a magnificent view; and the music to which you listen, as you make your way to the entrance, completes the allurement. What an evening! I had never seen a gambling-table before. I passed from one table to another and looked at the players, too intent on the game to notice us. All was still, — the only noise, the shovelling of the gold. I saw lovely looking women, old and young, at the tables; no excitement apparently. The excited ones were those who were looking on, many of them debating whether or not to risk a little, just to try it. I saw young girls drawn into this vortex for the first time, and you could see the colour come and go in their cheeks. But those at the table seemed to be beyond that. At eleven o'clock all must leave.

We lingered till near that time in the gardens, standing among the beautiful shrubbery, enjoying the air, so pure and fresh after that of the close, brilliantly lighted rooms. While standing thus, there came from the gambling-rooms a well-dressed lady, who quickly passed by us into the dense shrubbery. In an instant there came to our ears a cry of despair which none who heard will ever forget. She threw herself on the ground, and again and again we heard the heart-rending cry. A man emerged from under some trees and lifted her up; but she extricated herself from his grasp and again threw herself on the ground with that shriek of despair. In a few minutes all was still. She had gone or was carried away, whither no one knew. It confirmed all I had heard of Monte Carlo, — a paradise with a serpent in it. The woman had evidently lost all.

The next day we drove from Nice to Monte Carlo, over the famous drive of the world, — the Corniche Road. In a jeweller's shop at Monte Carlo we were shown a beautiful necklace of pearls that were for sale. They were left to pay some gambling debt, the jeweller said, and the owner, a lady, was waiting till the pearls were sold in order to get to her home. She had no money to get away. The old story, — " the pleasures of sin for a season," and the season soon over. After the night when I heard that woman scream, I did not care to see the beauty of the place. We drove over to Monaco, the seat of the prince of that name. It is situated on a bold rocky promontory one mile from Monte Carlo. The prince derives his

vast revenues from the great gambling
establishment.

At Nice we saw the famous Battle of
the Flowers. This fête was new to me,
although I had seen carriages as beautifully decorated at the Flower Festival in
the White Mountains. We had front seats
on the grand stand before our hotel, where
we could see it all. One of our party
had provided herself with six hundred
bouquets; but four hundred more were
needed before the battle was over. The
carriages contained huge baskets filled
with flowers; bouquets were thrown to
the spectators ; and, as quick as a flash, the
compliment was returned. I could not
help thinking how much lovelier it was to
throw flowers than stones. Ah, we need
more battles of flowers, even in our fami-
lies ! Those who threw the most received
the most; those who threw sparingly

received sparingly. I noticed that it was not always the most beautifully decorated carriages that were bombarded, or the most elegantly dressed women who had the best time, but rather those who gave the most.

I am sorry I can say so little of what the truly religious or Christian people may be doing in this and that place; but we passed so quickly from one point to another, simply getting a bird's-eye view of all, that I really had no time to make any extended investigation. I had to be content with the loving souls with whom I found myself face to face as the days went by. We saw only enough to make us hungry to see more; maybe life itself is only to create hunger for the more beautiful beyond. I once met a lovely woman who said life was only just long enough for you to make your selections, and in the Great Beyond you would have time to cultivate what you selected here. So far as drives are concerned, I should select that drive in the most pict-uresque and beautiful portion of the Riviera. It winds along the coast, in and out among the bold promontories that jut out into the sea, promontories all covered with most luxuriant vegetation.

WE are now back again on our steamer. The two days at Tunis were memorable days. In the morning, when we were ready to go on shore, there was a commotion in the companion-way, and we learned that our stewardess, who had greeted us, only a little while before, with her pleasant smile, had fallen and was being carried to the officer's room. She had said to one of the other maids, only a few moments before, " My morning's work is nearly done; I have only a few more ladies to wait on." How little she knew how nearly done it was! The doctor said it was heart disease. In a short hour all was over. We stepped

24

into our row-boat. She was carried in another. Who could have foreseen, that morning when she served us in our state-room, what would happen in such a short time? All the stewards and employees on the boat raised a fund, not only for covering her grave with flowers, but for the erection of a stone to mark her rest-ing-place in the Protestant burial-ground, where is buried the one who wrote " Home, Sweet Home."

Some time afterwards, on making in-quiries about her, I found that she was not at all well when she engaged for the voyage, and her friends had done all they could to get her to take a rest. But she was a widow with an only son, and her answer was, " The boy must be educated, and I must earn the money." In the pocket of her dress was found a letter from her boy, who was at school in

Switzerland, I think. He asked his
mother if she could spare him two shil-
lings. A well-known man of our country
started a subscription list, and enough
money was subscribed to educate the boy.
Oh, the unwritten histories ! I could only
imagine that mother's anxiety for her
fatherless boy, her own efforts, and all
her patient toil till she fell. Then, in a
way she had never dreamed of, her
prayers were answered. Her boy would
be educated. It seemed that the death
of the mother would do more for the
boy than her life could have done. In
that hour the Fatherhood of God and
the possible brotherhood of man seemed
more within reach.

I saw and had a conversation with the
Lutheran minister who buried the " Smiling Stewardess " (as we called her), and
he told me he was engaged in building

a little church, to be called " The Home, Sweet Home Church." (I wish all the churches were real " Home, Sweet Home churches.")

Here at Tunis, we saw the Palace of the Bey, and we went through the Harem. The Bey was absent with his wives. Of course, the chief attraction is a visit to the site of ancient Carthage. Hardly anything remains intact but the cisterns, still capable of holding water. The ruins are truly melancholy. It was our return to the steamer that marked the day. The sea had become rough, and there was difficulty ; the landing certainly looked dangerous to those standing on the steamer watching for the boats to come in. The distance was much greater from the steamer to the shore at Tunis than at any other place ! The waves ran so very high ! The boat in which I sat was the

last of a number of boats, so the interest
was intense. The only way for us to
board the steamer was to step on the
little platform, on which rested the ladder
that ran down the side of the steamer,
just as the wave lifted the boat to the
platform. You had to be careful so as not
to step before or after. There was just
one moment in which it could be done.
The officer had his hand extended, and if
you took advantage at the right instant, all
was well; but if there was the slightest
hesitation, there was only one way, and
that was to drag you up, and I had seen
more than one pulled up just as the wave
was taking the boat back. As I rose in
the boat, I heard a stranger say as I took
up my wrap, " Leave all," so I threw the
wrap down in the boat, and as the boat
lifted, stepped on to the platform. After
my return home I heard that I had

fainted and was dragged on the ship, but there was not the slightest truth in that. I never was calmer or less in danger of fainting, though it was an exceedingly trying moment; but my friend, who watched it all from the deck of the steamer, suffered far more than I did, for, by chance, I was the only one of our party on the boat. The others had come by a previous boat, and had landed on the other side of the ship, where there was less danger. As I look back at it all now, I could hardly afford to lose it out of the trip. It is a nice thing to step just at the right moment, not too soon, not an instant too late. It made me think of lines I have never seen in print:

" God's wisdom is immense ;
His heart profoundly kind,
God never is before His time,
And never is behind."

How unlike Him are we! How apt to be behind or before!

I think that picture will be a great help to me in my inner life. Fortunes have been lost by not taking a step when a hand has been outreached. How well I remember keeping my eye on the officer whose hand I was to take! The waves had lifted the boat so that I could step. It was no time to look at the waves or at those who were watching from the deck of the ship. I simply had to step — and there was the hand. How vivid it all is now as I write! It illumines such words as, "*Now* is the accepted time," "*Now* is the day of salvation." The Holy Ghost saith *now*.

Another wave lifted me on a level with the platform. How often I have seen souls lifted by the waves of deep feeling, knowing that the ship of safety must be reached ; and yet at the moment they must take the step of faith, they allow themselves to be swept back. "And they entered not." Why? Because they feared — they doubted. Many a step we would take, if we but listened to the words of warning, —

> " To doubt would be disloyalty,
> To falter would be sin.''

When the step is taken which lands us not in the arms of earthly friends merely, but in the everlasting arms, and we are greeted by the Captain of our Salvation and congratulated on our safety — this is bliss indeed. And with such a Captain, and in the company of those with us in the ship, we are ready for any calm or storm that may be ahead of us, before we drop anchor on the far shore, where, whatever the words may mean, whether of mystery or separation, "there shall be no more sea ! "

THERE is a peculiar interest to me in visiting the island of Malta, aside from my desire to see an old friend who resides on the island, and of whose beautiful home I had so often heard, and now hope to have the pleasure of visiting. It was off this island that the vision of the angel came to Saint Paul. It was there he said of God, " whose I am and whom I serve," — a word I have need to remember in these days of travel, for travelling, even in Bible lands, does not necessarily make you spiritual ; indeed, it is just the reverse. There is so much to attract the attention and dissipate the thought, that unless you see the things

that are not seen, while looking at the
things that are temporal, you can become entirely worldly. On the very spot
almost where Saint Paul was shipwrecked,
you will find yourself gazing at laces and
silks curiously woven, and you will think
of this one and that one to whom you
would like to take these things, forgetting
that they could not be much to others
without the associations. Yet there is
another side, and I really feel indebted to
a gentleman who said to me a few minutes
ago, when I told him I feared I should
backslide, going into the shops and looking at the curious things and wanting to
buy what I did n't need: " Do you
ever think that in buying you are keeping people from starvation? This is
the mission of these people; they are
taught of God to make the Maltese lace;
and if there was no one to buy it, what

3   33

would become of them?" I realized in that conversation with a thoughtful man, the truth of the old word, "The merchandise of it [of wisdom] is better than the merchandise of silver, and the gain thereof than fine gold." He helped me, and showed me, what I was in danger of forgetting, that "as God has given some of us money, we are responsible for giving it; while others who have not that mission must look out that in no way they dim the fine gold of thought and inspiration God has given them." A conversation like the one I had with this same gentleman made me think that we so seldom give this exchange of our best thoughts to one another.

But I had commenced to tell you about Malta. We were fortunate in being there on the first day of Lent, and we heard a part of the sermon preached by the

Bishop of Malta (alas ! we did not understand a word of what he said) in the
famous Church of St. John. This
church was constructed by the Knights
of Malta, and because the Maltese cross
that we wear as members of the order of
The King's Daughters and Sons was their
symbol, I was especially interested in
learning all I could about these Knights.
The floor on which I stood while listen-
ing to the Bishop preach was inlaid with
some two hundred mortuary slabs in
memory of the Knights. They are very
quaint, and many of them curiously beautiful. The order was, as perhaps you
know, both military and religious. The
church is surmounted by a Maltese
cross, beneath which is a figure of our
Saviour. I was most interested in going
down, not long afterwards, into a crypt,
or chapel, and finding myself surrounded

by all that was left of the bodies of two
thousand of the Knights of Malta.
Their skulls are curiously arranged in
figures, and the bones of their arms made
to form the Maltese cross. Under the
altar in Latin we read these words: *The
world is a theatre, and human life is a per-
sonification of vanity. Death breaks in and
dissolves the illusion, and is the boundary of
all worldly things. Let those who visit
this place think on these maxims. Pray for
perpetual rest to the dead lying herein, and
carry with you a lovely remembrance of
death. Peace be with you.* We said
" Amen " as we turned away, leaving the
bones of the brave Knights behind us.
Their life had been very stormy, and we
were glad to think of them as at rest.

We did not care to see in one of the
chapels above the altar a thorn which was
said to be a portion of the crown of

thorns worn by Christ; nor a fragment of
the cradle of the infant Jesus, nor one of
the stones which slew St. Stephen, nor sev-
eral other " sacred relics." We felt there
was much more need to be willing to be
thorn-crowned ourselves, and to have the
spirit of the Holy Child Jesus, and to be
careful we did not throw stones at any of
the living saints. We were told that the
crucifix over the altar was made from the
basin used at the washing of the disciples'
feet. How much easier it is to worship
in the letter rather than in the spirit!
And yet the Master's words so plainly
spoken are, " God is a spirit, and they who
worship Him must worship Him in
spirit and in truth." But after all, the
interest in the island is associated with
Saint Paul. No one, I think, can doubt
but that here is the spot spoken of in the
first verse of the 28th chapter of Acts:

" And when they were escaped, then they knew that the island was called Malta (Melita)." It is certainly a place where two seas meet, " a creek with a shore." I certainly felt that I was on sacred ground.

In 1845 a white statue of the Apostle was erected, visible far to seaward, and it requires but little imagination to picture the truly grand old man standing on the deck of that stranded ship, calmer and more self-possessed than any experienced sailor of that shipwrecked company. One is glad to think that Saint Luke was with him. There is a statue also of the beloved physician not far away from that of Saint Paul. Ah, Saint Paul was *the* Knight of the Cross ; all other Knights pale before that hero of the Cross of the Crucified One.

CAN it be possible I am in Egypt? We approached the mysterious land on the morning of the 21st of February. The blue Mediterranean never looked half so blue as it did that morning, and the sunlight on the white shores of Egypt made a picture never to be forgotten. It was a fitting close of our radiant voyage on the beautiful Mediterranean.

Soon the row-boats were on their way to us. We were not in Cook's party, so we were not on the side of the ship where the great crowd was. Our courier was on the lookout for Mr. Clark's agent. We easily distinguished him by the

American flag which he carried. Then
ensued a scene beyond all description for
wildness. The "children of the desert"
are by no means so quiet as is the desert.
I never heard such a babel of voices in
all my life, and I knew the meaning of
"fleet of foot" as I saw these Arabs,
carrying our trunks, run down the ladder with a swiftness that was bewildering.
I could quite understand their running
before the chariots.

What we should have done without
Mr. Valentine, our courier, I could not
say, for he could shout in Arabic with
the best of them. Shephard's was over-
crowded, so we drove to the Continental,
where rooms were waiting for us, and we
soon found ourselves in a most delightful
hotel. If we had wished to see titled
people, the Duke of Cambridge and other
notable people could be seen at the hotel.

I shall always remember that four
hours' railway journey from Alexandria
to Cairo. The palms could be seen in
the moonlight, and occasional white
houses of some kind or other; but it
was a desert-looking place, and as I
looked out of the window of the car, I
could see in imagination the blessed
Mother with the Child in her arms, fleeing into Egypt, — that Babe, the hope
of the world. And so many old words
had such a new meaning as I said over
and over to myself, " I am in Egypt ! "
" Out of Egypt have I called my Son."
The old Bible stories of my childhood
came back to me, and the weird strains
of another dark race, singing, " Let my
people go." Everything is fascinating
to me. The figures in vari-coloured
costumes, in our hotel, or flitting in
and out among the palms that are every-

where, made a variety of pictures. The white and sky-blue of their robes, the variety of colours in their turbans, all formed a moving panorama. I had thought I had seen black people, but I never saw anything so black as these Nubians.

As I opened my Bible this morning I read, " Fear not to go down into Egypt; . . . I will go down with thee into Egypt; and I will surely bring thee up again." This word was given me by a friend as I left New York, but it means more than ever to me this morning. I was sorry we could not have stopped in Alexandria for a few hours on our way to Cairo. It was in this city, founded by Alexander the Great, that the Old Testament was translated into Greek from the Hebrew, receiving the name of the Septuagint from the fact that threescore and ten pious scholars, called " The Seventy," were engaged in the work. But we were eager to get our letters, and though our trip means more to us than those trips that are described as "rushing through Europe to get letters from home," yet we were very desirous to hear from home.

AND now shops, bazaars, mosques!
Nearly two thousand of them, I
learn. The distant pyramids! The
famous museums! All to be visited
immediately!

Undoubtedly the best way is to take
a carriage, or walk out and stroll, and
take in, for the first time, Oriental life
in this way. I saw that morning, for
the first time, the running footmen.
Never could I have imagined such graceful movements. No person of position
drives in Cairo without one or two of
these attendants. The "sais," they are
called. They are young and handsome,
gorgeously attired, and wear skull-caps.
I learned afterwards, they die young;

44

the pace kills them. I could seem to see one of these running footmen before Ahab's chariot.

The scene in the streets, or alleys, where the shops are, beggars description. It seemed as if every nationality were represented. How the donkeys could get through streets where there did not seem to be room for more than two persons to walk abreast, was surprising. We did not spend much time in the shops ; we wanted to see the pyramids.

You get the first glimpse of the pyramids from the windows of the railway carriage, — as you come from Alexandria ; but at that distance you are not impressed by their size. You do not feel as you do when you see the Alps for the first time ; but when you get to them, the effect is wonderful. Oh, the awful shadow the great pyramid casts !

It shuts out everything. That one pyramid is all you can see. We all have read that hundreds of years ago the great pyramid was stripped of the outer blocks to build Arab mosques and palaces; that accounts for its un-finished look.

The gentlemen of our party ascended that awful staircase, but we women did not. For we took no chances during our travels, and that is one reason, perhaps, why we returned in such vigorous phys-ical condition. I should have liked to see the colour of the pyramid in a certain light when, I am told, it looks like a pile of gold. Perhaps to be told that it stands one hundred and sixteen feet higher than the top of St. Paul's dome gives some idea of its size; but to stand up against it was an experience. I thought, when looking at the Sphinx, of the story I heard, that it never spoke but once, and that was when Ralph Waldo Emerson stood before it. Then the stone lips moved, and Emerson heard the words, "You're another!"

Here on the desert I had my first experience with a race for which I was prepared at least to have respect. To be sure, I had had no personal knowledge of camels till that day. The largest camel was selected for me; why, I cannot imagine! The great creature crouched down and the dragoman lifted me on its back. The camel gave such a howling groan as I did not wish to hear repeated; but I thought it was because he would have liked a lighter load. But he gave the same awful groan when I was taken off, and looked at me afterwards. That look took away all respect I ever had for camels; for he plainly

showed he had no respect for me. That
look seemed to say: "Why are you
here? You are too young to look at."
The camel looked as if he were a thousand years old. I am sorry to have to
say all this, but it is true. And what
with that look and the groaning, I made
up my mind it belonged to a race of
grumblers. I do not say camels have
nothing to grumble about; but they
grumble when they have no cause for
grumbling, and grumbling is a very bad
thing. That was the trouble with the
children of Israel, in the very land I
had gone to see. "Their carcasses fell
in the wilderness" because of grumbling;
they "murmured"; that is, grumbled.

I had my picture taken while I was
on that very camel. In the picture I
have a placid look. Why, I shall never
he able to understand; for I think I

never was more frightened in my life than when on that camel. When that great creature moved with a groan, and I went up, up, and did not know how much higher I might go, I assure you, although I have been very fond of saying " Look up and not down," at this time I did not want to look up. I looked down and reached down, and said to the dragoman and another Egyptian standing by, " Oh, keep hold of my hands ! " and then came another of those awful groans ! I was thoroughly scared !

I did take a short ride on the dreadful creature afterwards, just to be able to say I had done it (I doubt whether that thing ever pays !), but it was my last as well as my first ride on a camel. I am sorry my dream about camels is dispelled ; but ever since then I have had to count them out of my objects of admiration.

OUR boat! I may have joy in many boats in the future, but I shall take no such interest in any as I did in this, which was all our own. Our House Boat, — what a haven it was to us the night we foolishly walked from the station to it instead of taking the donkeys!

The morning following, I saw a sunrise on the Nile, a picture that will stay with me for ever! How we enjoyed being by ourselves! We hardly condescended to notice the dahabiyehs that passed us filled with other tourists. There was a strange fascination in being on the Nile, where it never rains, and where the sun always shines; and yet for all the beauty of the

50

moonlight night on the lovely Nile (which I cannot begin to describe) Egypt seemed like one vast graveyard.

One experience on our boat is noted in my diary, which has this record: " *Out of our course.*" Yes, we were on a sand-bank. I looked at other boats, dahabi-yehs that were in their course, as they sailed by; but we were on a sand-bank. How well I remember the welcome words, " *We're off!* " that at last greeted us. We had been disappointed again and again; had thought more than once we were really moving: but now there was no doubt of it; we were in deep water again. There are many people who are out of their course, and are on a sand-bank. There are people who steer according to the " course of this world," and they are satisfied to stay on their little sand-bank. Their God is the God of this world, and they wish for no other. The saints of old were quite bewildered with the prosperity of such, and did not at first see that they were in slippery places. And there are others who start on another course, with a purpose to come to their best; and they make mistakes, and find themselves out of their course and on a sand-bank. Now, apart from all the chances that brought them there, and all the helps that at last made them move into deeper water, it is a very pleasant cry to hear resound within to the ear of the soul, as well as it was to us in our difficulty, — "*We 're off!*" How pleasant it was just to know that we were moving! Safety is to be sought in the mid-stream.

HOW the tall form and intelligent face of our dragoman stands before me now, and I can hear his voice in the tombs at Thebes, calling our especial attention to the figures and scenes on the walls. He was quite silent as he rode by my side that day on our way to the tombs. I think the only time he spoke to me was when he said of the little Mohammedan girl, " She has no mother " ; but I talked to him in the tombs that day as he explained everything. Imagine my surprise at hearing him say, " Madame, here is a four o'clock tea " ; and sure enough, cut in the stone was a little table, and not only the cups and saucers, tea-pot, sugar-bowl, and milk-jug, but even the biscuits. This was done four thousand years ago, and the faces of the ladies did not seem unlike faces you meet on Fifth Avenue.

In this tomb I saw more symbols of the one doctrine which lived, we are told, persistently and unchanged, in the Egyptian mind for five thousand years: the doctrine of the future life. So much was symbolical of the resurrection. Indeed, the grand tombs themselves were not built as mere objects of pride, but as everlasting habitations which would preserve the body from decay and keep it ready to be reinhabited by the soul at the proper season.

But at last I became tired of the perpetual, "This is the god so and so, and this is the god of that and that," and I exclaimed, "Oh, mercy! they have a god for everything, have they not?"

"Oh, yes," he said, "for everything."

"But there is only one God," I exclaimed very earnestly. Then the face of our dragoman lighted up as he said, "There is only one God"; and I knew what he was going to add, so I shook my head, smiling, and repeated, "There is only one God," and, "Thou shalt have no other gods before Me." He smiled as I passed on with him, repeating to myself, "I am the Lord thy God."

How surpassing strange it has been, day after day, to look at so much that is four thousand years old! I am quite used to the words, "*so* many years before Christ." I am bewildered with the oldness of everything. I sit on the deck of our boat and see them drawing up water from the Nile just as it was drawn

up four thousand years ago. This wonderful Nile! The ancient Egyptians rec-
ognised how very much they owed to
the Nile, and in their hymns they thank
the Nile-god in appropriate and grateful
terms. Statues of the god are painted
green and red, which colours are supposed
to represent respectively the bright green
colour of the river in June before the in-
undation, and the ruddy hue which the
water has when changed by the red mud
brought down from the Abyssinian mountains. The river has a strange fascination for me. It makes Egypt. In all
the marvellous tombs of the kings, everywhere, you see the Nile cut in the stone,
and the sacred boat on the sacred river.

It was a never-ending source of wonder
to me that the colours could retain their
brilliancy after so many thousands of
years. You see the same beautiful green

of the Nile in the representations of the
sacred serpent, which also is graven on
all the tombs. I saw so many of the
kings' heads crowned with the serpent.
The sculpture in these tombs is wonderful. Usually it symbolises the life of
the kings. Now and then some sym-
bolic picture in the tombs gave to the
words in our New Testament a new sig-
nificance. I saw one of the gods offer-
ing the water of life, and the words of
Christ came so freshly to my mind : " If
any man thirst, let him come unto Me
and drink." Another symbol was the
tree of life. How real it was to me, that
what they were groping after we have in
our glorious gospel !, The sun-god was
on every wall, but the warm healing rays
of the Sun of Righteousness they did not
know.

I can see now why Egypt has been

used by Christians as a symbol of unregenerate nature. Yet in its unregenerate
state there is the longing for a better life,
the need of worship; and so we "fill these
lower courts with broken images of Him."
It is all so pathetic to me; at times I
cannot look at the misery, so often the
result of their dismal belief. The flies,
being considered sacred, never can be
brushed even from their eyes. Blindness
is therefore very common, and nothing
could be more pitiful than the suffering
of the little children, their eyes almost
covered with the flies.

How lovely our Christianity is by contrast! I cannot conceive of any one
visiting this land and not loving the
Founder of our faith more and more.
Yet, the Egyptian spirit is in our Christian land, and we have to fight idolatry
in ourselves. The words I heard so

often still ring in my ears,—"I am very
hungry, lady." At first I thought she
wanted something to eat. I had some
crackers in my pocket which I thought
she might like, for I knew it was the
time of the fast, so I handed the child
a cracker; but she said, "Oh, no, lady,
hungry for backsheesh." Ah, yes, hungry
for money. The one cry everywhere,
more money! I said to one of the girls
who put out her little brown hand and
cried, "Backsheesh,"—

"I did give you some money."

"Oh, yes," she said, "thank you, lady,
but more! more!"

I am glad we go from Egypt to the
Holy Land. "I would see Jesus"; and
yet the truth that I thought was real to
me is more real to me to-day. "The
Kingdom is within you." What we *are*,
not what we see! Man's happiness comes

never from without. All you get in
travelling is from what you carry with
you. The old truths will be wonderfully
illuminated for me by these journeyings
into new, distant lands.

In wandering among these ruins of
magnificent temples, you naturally think
of what they must have cost. Of course
it is impossible to estimate, but we are
told that every palace, every temple, represented a hecatomb of human lives. We
know how the Hebrews suffered, and yet
they were less cruelly used than some
who were kidnapped from beyond the
frontier. One can hardly endure the
thought of the suffering undergone by
those who laboured under ground, goaded
on, without rest or respite, till they fell
down in the mines and died. There are
lessons to be learned in this land of Egypt
for those who are studying the problems

of capital and labour. The Sermon on
the Mount is the solution of the social
problem.

The one central figure that is with you
all the time you are on the Nile, from the
hour when you saw him as a mummy in
the Museum in Cairo, is Rameses the
Second, the Pharaoh of the Captivity,
whose son and successor was the Pharaoh
of the Exodus. This, I believe, has
been settled. The Bible and the monuments confirm one another. One is always
sorry that Moses did not once call either
of the three Pharaohs by the cartouche
name, but I have read that they were not
allowed either to speak or write the names
of their kings. As I roam through these
ruins and imagine the glory, they seem
to me soaked with human suffering. As
I looked at the features of Rameses the
Second in the Museum at Cairo, I quoted

to myself the words, " There's nothing great but God " ; I said it again on the Nile ; I felt it more deeply still when I wandered through the ruins of the great temple he built, — the aisles of which undoubtedly Moses wandered through, and pondered in his heart the meaning of all this earthly grandeur, only the ruins of which we now see. He was a prince among princes, the adopted son of the king's daughter ; he knew how much of all this earthly magnificence would be his. As I walked over the ground where Moses walked, through those halls of ruined greatness, those words in the eleventh chapter of Hebrews never were more significant to me : He chose " rather to suffer affliction with the people of God, than to enjoy the pleasures of sin for a season ; esteeming the reproach of Christ greater riches than the *treasures in*

Egypt; for he had respect unto the recompense of the reward." And *he has it.*

What now is that mummy in the Museum, and his empty tomb on the Nile, and all these broken statues of the great king, compared with Moses, who gave the Ten Commandments from the hand of God to this sinful world? How wise Moses was to choose affliction with the people of God! All the interest we have to-day in these kings and tombs is that they prove the truth of what was written by Moses, the great law-giver of the world.

I would consider my visit to Egypt a failure did I not take in the inner truth taught me by all that I saw. It is certain that only character, only spirit, lives on. The tombs are being ransacked. The mummy is taken out to be exhibited, and one exclaims, " I have seen an end of hu-

man greatness." But the cross brightens
in the shadows, and you feel sure it will
triumph, because it is the power of love
in suffering; it is the laying down of life
for *others;* it is the eternal emblem of
voluntary self-sacrifice! I shall sing,

"In the cross of Christ I glory,
  Towering o'er the wrecks of time,'"

with a deeper meaning after my visit
to Egypt, and our trip up the Nile.

FAREWELL TO THE RUINS
OF EGYPT

A FRENCH writer has put Egypt in an epigram : "A donkey ride and a boating trip interspersed with ruins." Miss Edwards said that this sentence gave the whole experience of the Nile traveller, and added, apropos of these three things, the donkeys, the boat, and the ruins: " It may be said that a good English saddle and a comfortable dahabiyeh add very considerably to the pleasure of the journey, and that the more one knows about the past of the country the more one enjoys the ruins." The first two, the saddle and boat, we had; but, speaking only for myself, I was not well read up

on the ruins, so I cannot say with Miss
Martineau that I was not satisfied to sit
down to breakfast without having first
explored a temple; much less could I
say with Miss Edwards, "I could have
breakfasted, dined, and supped on temples." She says her appetite for them was
insatiable, and grew with what it fed on.
To tell the truth, I became tired of them
after I had seen the greatest of them ; but
we were unfortunate in being at Luxor
and Karnak in extremely hot weather.
To be sure we did not have to walk ; we
had our donkeys. Among the ruins at
Karnak, — and they were the grandest by
far, — the temple where undoubtedly
Moses walked, the temple built by
Rameses the Second, the Pharaoh of
Moses' time, was the most interesting to
me. At Karnak, after looking again at
the kings and the gods and goddesses

sculptured in the walls and looking up
and down the vast aisles of pillars (one
hundred and thirty in that temple, each
one measuring eleven yards around), I felt
like singing (and we did), —

> " My country, 'tis of thee,
> Sweet land of liberty,
> Thy name I love.
> I love thy rocks and rills,
> Thy woods and *templed* hills."

I seem to see in these temples the Hebrew
children making bricks without straw;
and the unwritten history of millions
of sufferers. In the ruins of the temple at Karnak, I saw little boys not
over twelve years of age carrying great
stones for one piastre a day (five cents
of our money). The excavations are
going on. I looked at five of the sacred
bulls which have been unearthed during
the year; and every day discoveries are
being made.

A Sunshine Trip

There is no end of tombs. Egypt seems a vast sepulchre beneath our feet. In going to the temple yesterday, we passed through a very long avenue of palms, with the lesser sphinxes on either side which have been unearthed recently. There seems also no end to the sphinxes. I wish I had seen the picture a well-known writer speaks of. She says : " You see in the picture a brown, half-naked, toil-worn fellah laying his ear to the stone lips of a colossal sphinx buried to the neck in sand. Some instinct of the old Egyptian blood tells him the creature is godlike. He is conscious of a great mystery lying far back in the past. He has perhaps a dim, confused notion that the big head knows it all, whatever it may be ; he fancies those closed lips might speak if questioned. Fellah and sphinx are alone together in the desert.

It is night, and the stars are shining. Has he chosen the right hour? What does he seek to know? What does he hope to hear? Under the picture you read, —

> "Each must interpret for himself
> The secret of the sphinx."

How glad I am that our God is not silent to us! He does speak to us. We do hear His voice, and we not only have a God that knows, but one that loves. I hoped that I should get from this trip an illuminated Bible, and I am getting it.

"Come this way," our dragoman called out yesterday in the temple at Karnak, "and see the tree of life." As I stepped along over the stones the words came so vividly to my mind that I repeated them as I looked up at the sculptured tree with one of the gods in the centre of it: "And on either side of the river was

there the tree of life." Then he directed
our attention to one of the gods pouring
out the water of life. I shook my head
as I said, " If any man thirst, let him
come unto *Me* and drink " ; " I am the
water of life."

I was reading a long letter to one of
our party afterwards. I had been writing
and giving my reflections while in that
same temple; our dragoman was leaning
up against the side of the boat, and I discovered that he was an attentive listener.
When I read, " I am God, and beside Me
there is none else," I happened to look
up, and the bright smile was on his intelligent face. I smiled and said, "One God!"
and added : " You are my Mohammedan
brother and I am your Christian sister.
We may not see alike here " (laying my
hand on my head), " but God looks here,"
I said (as I laid my hand on my heart).

He smiled, as in his broken English he said, " Ah, yes, you are right ! "

While we were there, quite a procession passed through the temple, singing. I asked the dragoman what they were saying, and he replied that they were praying to the prophet. " Praying to the prophet ! " I said : " Are they priests ? " " Oh, no, only the workingmen. They say, ' Allah, help us ! oh, help us ! ' " These people affect me. The more I see of them, the more they appeal to my pity.

On our way home we rode through an Arab village. The street was so narrow I could see the faces of the people at their work. Of course they are noisy; but they strike me as being innocent and harmless. I said to our dragoman who was riding at my side : " Where are the rich people ? All I see are so poor." He replied, " There are only one or two in

a place; all the rest are poor, very poor."
A few minutes after a fine turn-out passed
us, — two gentlemen. One was the son of
the French consul; he is a captain, and for
the second time I saw the graceful runner
who runs before the carriage. Never
could I have imagined such gracefulness,
such fleetness. Once again the sight of
the runner makes so life-like certain Old
Testament scenes. But one can only feel
pity for the men who must thus earn their
daily bread. The abject misery of the
poorer classes is pitiable. No wonder their
constant cry is, " Money ! " Why is it, I
have so often asked myself, where one sees
the greatest beauty of architecture, one sees
the poorest specimens of humanity? The
great cathedrals of Europe impoverished
the people of the places where they were
built, and the contrast between the ruins
of these magnificent temples and the utter

poverty of the people never ceases to impress me.

We're off! Such a clapping of hands and such glad shouting on Sunday the first of March, as we found ourselves moving off the sand-bank where we had been stranded for twenty-four hours! " Out of our course," " shallow water," and like expressions, had a significant meaning for me. When night came, and I could hear the voices of the Arabs busy at work trying to get us off the sand-bank, I went into my state-room and took up my Bible with a hope that God would speak to me through the sacred Word., I had seen so many things that were called sacred : " sacred river," " sacred serpent," " sacred eye," " sacred boat " ; everything sacred, but not making the worshippers sacred ; an utter absence of the Spirit. So to take up our " sacred book " was a joy ; and as I opened it my eyes fell on the words, "Thy thoughts are very deep." They had a fresh meaning because our trouble had been that we were not in deep water. So I had some profitable reflections during the time we were trying to get off the sand-bank. It is very easy to get out of a deep current, God's current; from God's deep thoughts into shallow streams, and on some sand-bank. But it is not so very easy to get off these sand-banks.

I see so many people in life who are evidently out of God's current; they have not taken their soundings, and so have drifted on to these sand-banks. A little distance from them you see other barks, not so valuable, perhaps, sailing along in the right current, as we saw boats through all those hours when we were not moving. The trouble with so many of us is that we do not keep in the current of God's thoughts. *They* are " *very deep*," but we drift into the shallow current of our own thoughts or other people's thoughts, and so we miss the grand sailing in God's deep river of thought.

So there was much of cheer in the two words, " *We're off!* " It was Sunday morning when we heard these cheering words, and I went to my state-room to get my Bible to have a little reading in the Old Testament. It is wonderful how illumined the Old Testament is now that I have seen the sculptured idols of all the Egyptians that God told His ancient people they should not worship. With what a new meaning Joshua's last charge to the children of Israel came home to me! God would not have them *speak* the names of these gods. (How tired I became of their names!) I think never did God's command, " Thou shalt have no other gods before me," sound so grand. We may well say, "Incline my heart to keep this law." It is no little thing to obey God. I realised it on this Sunday morning.

The word came that we were nearing one of the places where we were to see the ruins. If I had not seen any, and this was my only chance, I might have felt it was the right thing to do, but we had seen the greatest of them ; and while I know the difficulty there is in drawing the line, I do think that for those who profess to be serving God there should be at least one day sacred to Him, and that our Sunday should not be used for sight-seeing. There should be a Sabbath. What an example we had of this in the devout Mohammedans. How impressive it was to see those whose emblem is not the cross prostrate themselves at sunrise and sunset, no matter who happened to be near.

This morning I noticed our dragoman did not move while I sang, standing by the side of the boat, the entire hymn, " In the cross of Christ I glory " — and he understands English well. Oh, the difference it would make in this people if they only knew and followed Jesus Christ !

We are soon to be in the land of His birth, where He was " brought up," lived and died ; and yet His own words follow me, " The Kingdom is within you." It must be Christ in us. What a meaning will be connected with, " Ye are the temple of the living God," and " What ! know ye not your bodies are the temples for the Holy Ghost to dwell in ? " How full of instruction was everything I laid my eyes on, and I could not but call to mind that the Great Teacher drew His

deepest lessons from the commonest
things. As I looked at the forms being
unearthed, I thought of the buried souls
that need to emerge out of darkness into
God's marvellous light. Unearthed!
How significant the word sounded! I
stood close one day and saw one feature
after another come in sight. The workmen gathered around to see the sight;
for what was coming was of unusual
worth. I marked how careful the workman was who was using the instrument.
Oh, the infinite care, the infinite patience,
the Holy Spirit shows in His working
to restore the lost image! Maybe, if
we could see deeply enough, we should
see how much has to be removed in
order that the buried treasures may
come to light. I learned more than
one lesson as I stood and saw faces of
stone unearthed that afternoon.

I WANT to tell you of the little insect that has had so much greatness thrust upon it, and the lesson I learned from it, and how it reminded me of the real meaning of our order of "The King's Daughters." Perhaps you know about these scarabees. Every traveller on the Nile has had them offered to him for sale; perhaps genuine, more likely not. You have to buy them sooner or later to get rid of those who offer them. You know perhaps the history of this Egyptian insect.

A well-known writer says: "This beetle lays its eggs by the river's brink, encloses them in a ball of moist clay, rolls the ball to a place of safety on the

edge of the desert, buries it in the sand,
and when its time comes, dies content,
having provided for the safety of its
successors. Hence its mythic fame,
hence all the quaint symbolism that by
degrees attached itself to its little person and ended by investing it with a
special sacredness which has often been
mistaken for actual worship. Standing
by, and watching the movements of
the creature at its hard work of rolling
the burden up hill, its untiring energy,
its extraordinary muscular strength, its
businesslike devotion to the matter in
hand, one sees how subtle a lesson the
old Egyptian moralists had presented to
them for contemplation; and with how
true a combination of wisdom and poetry
they regarded this little black scarab, not
only as an emblem of the creative and
preserving power, but perhaps also of

the immortality of the soul. As a type,
no insect has ever had so much greatness thrust upon him. He became a
hieroglyphic, and stood for a word signi-
fying both 'to be,' and 'to transform.'
His portrait was multiplied a millionfold,
sculptured over the portals of temples,
fitted to the shoulders of a god, en-
graved on gems, moulded in pottery,
painted on sarcophagi and the walls of
tombs, worn by the living, and buried
with the dead."

I wish I had seen the living beetle at
its work; but the history of this beetle
made a great impression on me. I saw
it in every tomb I visited cut in the walls,
and I said over and over, if it had lived
for its own comfort and enjoyment, — in
short, if it had lived a selfish life, — it
would never have been known; and the
meaning of the word "others" in silver

on the ebony cross (a gift one of the lovely daughters of our Order gave me as I sailed away) had a deeper meaning for me. "Others!" He saved others. If any man will save his life, let him lose it, "and he that loseth his life for My sake, shall find it."

Did I tell you of a morning on the Nile when I rose very early, and, standing alone on our deck, looking at the shore of Egypt, I sang, —

"In the cross of Christ I glory,
   Towering o'er the wrecks of time."

My voice attracted our Mohammedan dragoman, and he stood near while I sang the whole hymn. Then I turned and said to him, "The cross will win, it will conquer; not the crescent, for the cross means *love*, self-sacrificing love." Somehow I think he will remember it. He smiled at me in his quiet way; but I

noticed afterwards that he always drew
near when I sang. He was very interesting to me ; he always lifted me on my
donkey as if I had been a baby. Oh, this
sad, sad Egypt, that I shall bid farewell
to for ever to-morrow ! I don't wonder
they took up the bones of Joseph and
carried them out of Egypt. I would not
like to be buried in Egypt. There was
nothing bright but its skies, its sunrising
and sunsetting.

I have become acquainted for the first
time with the Turks on this trip. They
are never far away from us. I am used
to seeing them at prayer, not only in their
mosques, but elsewhere. I was in Cairo
when their fast, answering to our Lent,
commenced, and I was in Jaffa, Palestine,
when it ended, and I saw them on Sunday,
their great feast day, answering to our
Easter, and for the first time they looked

happy. They were caring for us in so many ways during all their fast of forty days, and they never tasted food any of those days till after sundown. You know there are five commandments that Mahomet enforced on his followers. They must pray five times a day, bestow alms on the poor, perform the pilgrimage to Mecca, keep the fast of Ramazan, and observe bodily cleanliness as far as possible. This last commandment they did not seem to keep very strictly, for they never looked really clean.

In the Koran the prophet exhorts his followers to believe in one God, in the angels, in the other prophets (to the number of 124,000), and in *himself*, in the five books of Revelations, the Psalms, the Bible, the Koran, the resurrection of the dead, the last judgment, and the existence of heaven and hell.

I was surprised to know that they
believed that Abraham and King David
were Mohammedans; and the tomb of
Rachel is as sacred to a Mohammedan
as to a Jew or a Christian. They do not
believe in Jesus. Oh, how often, as I
have looked into the faces of the Mohammedan women, have I wished they
knew Jesus!

As there is a painful interest in the
Turks, — the unspeakable Turk, as we call
him just now, — you may want me to tell
you how they look and what seems to be
their character. Well, in the first place,
they always are lazy; they like to sit, as it
seemed to me, in thoughtless contemplation over their coffee and cigarette (perhaps we have some Turks in our country
that are called Christians). They always
seem serious to me. They are extremely
superstitious. I could tell you of the

strangest superstitions imaginable; for instance, they always keep their nails clean, because, if there is the least dirt in their nails, that implies unclean spirits. I wish some superstition would keep the whole body clean.

Of course you know they are fatalists. I never felt any fear of them, but we were never alone with them. Our courier was always with us; then we had our dragomans, and there was a gentleman in our party. The one thing they want is money, and they would only hurt themselves by harming us. And then they are under a chief, and are told what to do and what not to do. I must say I did not fall in love with them, but I did pity them.

ON the morning of February 27 we started soon after breakfast for a sight of the tombs of the kings, and for a visit to the great Rock Temple of Thebes. We crossed the Nile in a most ancient-looking boat, and the Arabs came walking in the water to carry us in their arms on shore. Slender-looking as these Arabs were, they took me up as if I had been a baby, and stood me on the bank where our donkeys were waiting for us. I was very glad the largest donkey was for me. Again I was lifted by our drago-man and put on the donkey's back as if I weighed only fifty pounds (my weight is considerably more). I looked at the

young Arab at the side of my donkey and
asked his name. He said his name was
Abraham, and the name of the donkey
was Rameses the First. Of course with
Abraham at my side, and on such a royal
donkey, I had no fear, and cantered off as
if I had been always used to donkeys (I
draw the line at camels); and so I took my
first donkey ride on the desert.

Shall I ever forget the touch of the little soft brown hand that rested on mine
as I rode on that donkey over the desert
to visit the kings' tombs? I did not see
the child till I felt the touch of her hand,
and, as I looked down, I saw that the soft
eyes of the little Egyptian girl were raised
to mine as she said, with the tender tones
peculiar to the children of the East (except when they are angry), "*I am your
daughter.*" "My daughter?" I said.
"Yes," she answered, "I am your daugh-

ter " ; and then she looked so tenderly into my face as she said, " Nice mother."

" And I am your mother ? " I inquired.

" Yes," she said, smiling, " nice mother. I am your daughter."

" Well, what is my daughter's name ? " I inquired.

" Amena," she answered.

" And you are my daughter Amena ? "

She laughed as again she said, " Yes, *nice mother.*"

Our dragoman, who was on the other side of me, said, " She has no mother ; her mother is dead ; she has only a father."

After that I looked more tenderly at the young girl, as she trotted by my side with her little feet bare, holding her water jar on her head ; so when the words came again, " Nice mother," they touched my heart.

I said to her, " And you have no mother ? "

Her face looked very sad as she shook her head and said, " No," and again came the words, " I am *your* daughter ; your daughter Amena."

I said, " Well, if you are my little Mohammedan daughter, then I must be your Christian mother." I did not know how the word " Christian " would strike her, but the same smile was on her face as she again said, " Nice mother."

Then I told her in simple language about a little daughter of mine whose name was Mamie, who had gone to live in a beautiful home with Jesus, the one who had said " Suffer the *little* children to come unto Me." I do not know how much she took in of what I said to her, but her face seemed so sad and interesting as it was lifted to mine, and her little brown hand nestled so closely in mine, that she seemed to understand. Just then some other girls of the same age ran up and said to me " Nice lady ! " Then Amena gave me such an imploring look, and turned almost savagely upon these girls, and getting closer to me said, " You know *I* am your daughter Amena," as much as to say, they only call you " Nice lady," — you are my " nice mother." Never did I see jealousy in a face more plainly than in that child's face.   Of course I did not forget that what she wanted was " backsheesh," but she had not uttered the word.

As we were nearing the tombs I put a coin in my daughter's hand, and she disappeared, and such a sudden disappearance I never saw ; if the earth had opened and swallowed her up, it could not have been more sudden.   I turned to the dragoman and said, " Well, my daughter has the money, and it seems as if that was

all she cared for, so she has disappeared."
So I did not expect to see my Mohammedan daughter again, but I must confess I was pleased on our return home
when she appeared again on the desert
with a fresh jug of water on her head, and
again I heard the words, " Nice mother,"
and " Thank you, mother," " You know I
am your daughter, your daughter Amena."
I was glad I had one little coin left, which
I put in her hand as I asked her where
she had been, and she said she had gone
home. A moment after she pointed to
her home. It was not so good as a pig-
sty, — a mud hut in which the owners and
their donkeys could lie down. Never
shall I forget that picture of utter deso-
lation — nothing but those mud holes did
I see, and these were called homes.

" *I am your daughter.*" Was she not
God's daughter ? Ah, me ! I often think

of my Mohammedan daughter in that
dreadful desert. She wears no silver cross
with "In His Name" on it, she is not on
the roll of The King's Daughters, and yet
somehow to me she is my Mohammedan
daughter, and what is far better, God's Mohammedan daughter. Years have passed
since I heard a minister say on a steamer,
"My poor Mohammedan brothers!" It
was the look on his face when he uttered
the words that made the words stay with
me. I understand him better to-day as I
say, "My poor Mohammedan daughter!"
Shall I never see her again? How I wish
I had done more for her; had even given
her more "backsheesh." I never can
think of any of the poor creatures to
whom I did not give any money, or gave
but little, that I do not regret not having given more. They are so wretchedly
poor! What we call poverty here is riches

compared with their condition. I know how hateful the name Mohammedan is to us, but I was taught a lesson I shall not soon forget when I heard an Armenian woman, whose relatives had been murdered by the Mohammedans, say, " Oh, we desire so that these Mohammedans should know our Lord Jesus ; we love their souls, and we hope that in seeing us die for the love of Christ, they may see that our Christianity is the true religion."

I turn from the picture of my Mohammedan daughter on the desert, with a prayer for more of the spirit of self-sacrifice that was in the Father of us all, who " so loved *the world* that He gave His only begotten Son." Do we love the whole world ?

CAIRO AFTER OUR RETURN FROM THE NILE

O N the morning of March the 2d we
were up at three o'clock, preparing
to take the five o'clock train from Girgeh
for Cairo. We breakfasted on our boat,
the " Elephantine," for the last time at
four o'clock. The beautiful moon enabled
us plainly to see our donkeys, and an
Egyptian cart on the shore waiting for
us. Ordinarily I should have preferred
to ride on the donkey, but the only chance
I should have of a ride in an Egyptian
cart was too great a temptation for me,
so I chose the cart. I had seen so many
veiled women on these carts (which had
for seats long boards with carpet thrown

over them). After that ride I could say I know how to *feel* for them, for that was certainly hard riding.

At five o'clock we were on our train, with all our baggage, including a very large basket of luncheon, for we had to travel all day again between two deserts. At six o'clock our dusty party arrived in Cairo, and then we learned the bad news that the cholera was in Cairo. We should have to be quarantined wherever we went, and we found that thousands were waiting to get out of Cairo. For a little time everything was so uncertain that I did not know but that I was going to miss seeing the Holy Land. For this I had come. Glad as I was of all that came to me on the way, still my heart had been set on seeing the land of His birth; the land where He worked, and suffered.

It took us all day to go from Cairo to

Port Said. We travelled through the Desert of Arabia, and it was refreshing to have our courier come to our window and point to Moses' Spring in the distance. We looked and saw some rocks quite a way off, and he told us that it was there that Moses smote the rock and a spring of water gushed out. Not long after we saw a sight most refreshing to see in a desert, — a small lake of water, which the guide said was the spot where Pharaoh was overthrown in the Red Sea; we certainly felt we were travelling over the land of the ancient story we knew so well. I got out of the cars and ran up a sandy hill to Abraham Heights, but before I had a chance to explore, the whistle blew, and I had to go back.

Now we were approaching what I wanted to see, — the Suez Canal. Never can I forget the sight. All I could think of was ships that sail in the desert. Very large ships they were; we saw five that were sailing along that blue canal. All the hopes, and the realisations of the hopes of different nations in having that canal finished, flashed upon the mind; the expense of it; the use of it; the sad history of the man associated with it, all come upon you so quickly. But the evening shut in on us, and looking out at the stars, and the lights that were becoming more and more distinct along the shore, we soon found ourselves at Port Said, where the yacht was waiting to take us to Beyroot, and in a few moments we bade farewell to the land of Egypt. We were very desirous to be off its shore, and we thought we could put up with any inconvenience if we were only free from Egypt.

MY first appearance in a mosque was in Algiers. I was, of course, interested in watching the Mohammedans at their devotions. It was a strange sight to me. I watched one man for a long time. The contrast between the Roman Catholic churches and the mosques are so great : the Mohammedans stand before the Invisible : no sign, no altars — no sound. I am sorry to say the look the man gave me when his eyes rested on me after his prayer, did not show that his religious exercises had improved his disposition, but I do not know that that fault is confined to Mohammedans. I have seen Christians whose dispositions did not seem improved by their religious exercises ; however, I don't think a Christian could have looked at me as that Mohammedan did. I was n't long in getting off my religious slippers after that. As a rule, the Mohammedans were exceedingly disagreeable to me; they were so dirty-looking, and yet their religion requires so much bathing. I could never help thinking what they would have been if they had not bathed so frequently.

How more and more precious our Christianity becomes at every step of the way! After we reached Egypt, we became quite used to the mosques. The day after we visited the great pyramid, we went to visit the mosque of Sultan Hassan, the most beautiful in Cairo, and perhaps the most beautiful in the Moslem world. It looks as if it would soon be a beautiful ruin. We are told that never in Cairo is anything repaired. New buildings go up, but no matter how venerable the old is — it is allowed to moulder away inch by inch till nothing remains but a ruin. Of course, before we entered the great court, we were obliged to put on the slippers.

There was a charming fountain in the court. It was all open to the sky, covered with prayer rugs, and there was a pulpit in the centre, and under the pulpit I saw a man that I was told had come to stay during the forty days' fast, and in that time he would eat nothing. All who came here seemed to come to pray, but you must remember these mosques are places of rest and refuge. Beside a man prostrate in prayer, I saw another man sewing buttons on his coat. It was new to me then that the Moslems are as devout out of the mosque as in it — (the good ones). Are all Christians as devout out of church as in it?

THE sixth of March finds us again on the blue Mediterranean. Undoubtedly, the inner history, the unwritten history, is by far the most important in our eyes. Shut up alone in that stateroom (my friends not knowing then of my sore throat), with the fever on me, I did not know but that my condition might be very serious. We were nearing Palestine, the land I had come so far to see, and I did not know what was before me ; it was one of the loneliest hours of my life, — spirit loneliness. And into the darkness and loneliness the living Christ came and said, " Without

Me ye can do nothing." When all the
memory of my trip to the East, when all
the outward, in a coming hour, shall have
faded from my mind, "without Me"
will still remain.

It was my preparation for the Jerusalem that was not to be what I had
dreamed. It was my preparation for
my disappointment at not seeing so much
I came to see; but yet I was not to be
" without Him," and that, after all, was
everything. So among all the blessings
of my trip, I must never forget the blessing in disguise of my illness on that yacht,
" The Norse King."

I little thought when I stepped on
that boat how eventful it would be to
me; but, alas! it was more eventful, in
a different way, to others whom we left
behind us on it, when our journey was
over. For, a few days after we left, it

was wrecked on the rocks, and the passengers were given only ten minutes to make their escape, losing all their luggage and the memorabilia of their trip.

My entrance into the Holy Land, lying in the compartment of the car on our way from Joppa to Jerusalem, was so different from what I had expected! I could hear them talking of all the places so familiar to a Bible student; but I, with my sore throat, was unable either to speak or lift up my head. Alas! for all my dreams of being really in the Holy Land. Still, before leaving for Jerusalem, I did manage to see a little of the ancient Joppa (now called Jaffa).

What will it matter to us that Peter had a vision, if we have none? The question asked by "our Henry," "Is this the place where we shall see visions?" stays with me. If we have the spirit that

Saint Peter had, we shall see visions. And even if old, we shall have our dreams, for the promise runs, "Your young men shall see visions, and your old men shall dream dreams."

I DO not wonder that Spurgeon never could be persuaded to visit the Holy Land. He feared that the sight of so much that was far from sacred would jar painfully on his cherished impressions of the land where our Saviour lived and died. I can quite understand him ; the mixture of all that is sacred to you with so much superstition is a great shock. I wanted to get away from the city ; I wanted to get to the Mount of Olives and to Bethany, for our Lord's ministry was almost wholly an out-of-door ministry. He taught in the open air ; and I was glad there was another spot in Jerusalem beside the one in the Church of the Holy

Sepulchre, where many think our Lord was crucified; they call the spot Gordon's Calvary, or Gordon's Golgotha. General Gordon made a very thorough study of this matter, and decided for himself that the hill outside the city was Calvary; and very strangely the spot is the shape of a skull. The Moslems own it, and have enclosed it; but no kind of building is on it. There it stands, — a green hill " outside the city wall."

The English, at a great cost, have recently bought the fields that surround it, and have put no building on it, I am thankful to say. You shrink so from seeing ordinary buildings on spots that are sacred. If I lived in Jerusalem that place would be Calvary to me; and I found that a number of those I met in Jerusalem go to that spot. You can see it from any part of the city. As you pass through the

Damascus gate, it seems the most natural distance and the way the sad procession would have passed. I am so glad I have a Calvary I shall love to think of. There was no satisfaction to me in the Calvary inside the church. I took comfort in the thought that Mary did not kiss the stone on which they say the angel sat, after His resurrection. She wanted to hear what the angel had to say. I did not kiss it, I did not kiss any stone; and I am sure Mary was too anxious about the risen Christ to stay any time in the sepulchre. She wanted *Him*, and so did I. Never did I appreciate the fact that I had a loving Christ so much as I did among the mummeries and superstitions connected with the life and death of our Lord, in the Church of the Holy Sepulchre. I still think if I could have gone to the Sea of Galilee and to the Jordan, of which I only caught sight from the Mount

of Olives, I might have had my dream of
Palestine realised. But that was denied
me, so I have my dream.

But do not think that my visit to the
Holy Land was a failure. It was not; I
saw things that are not seen, and they are
eternal; I saw things that will make me
a more serious woman for the rest of my
days. I saw that walking over the path
called the Via Dolorosa, "the sorrowful
way," does not necessarily bring you
nearer the Crucified One. And I saw
that we can never understand or appreciate His "sorrowful way" till *we* have a
Via Dolorosa, — a sorrowful way ourselves
to pass. Then, if we are willing, and
even glad to suffer for Him who suffered
for us, we are on the path He trod; and
there can be no real appreciation even of
the cross until we are crucified, until we
know something of the meaning of volun-

tary self-sacrifice. The religion of Jesus
is very costly, and that is the reason why
it will endure, and why His kingdom will
have no end.

Never did pride of every sort seem so
utterly out of place as in the Holy Land.
I saw a poor Russian peasant throw what
I still think was his last coin in that cave
of the Holy Sepulchre. He had kissed
the stone again and again, and finally threw
his body upon it. Then he had to leave;
but he turned back and threw the little
silver coin, and disappeared through that
door, to pass through which you literally
have to stoop down in order to get into
the cave. He was followed by a sleek
ecclesiastic; and the guide at my side said,
" These Greek priests fatten on the money
of these poor Russians." Oh, how much
rather in that moment would I have been
that poor peasant than the richest ecclesi-

astic ! I thought of a sentence I had
read : " Simple women have kept the piety
of the Church fragrant, when famous eccle-
siastics have trafficked with gold. Gener-
ous hearts have sheltered a homeless
Christ in the poor and little children,
although they wrote no epistles for after
ages."

Never did it seem so undesirable to be
rich as it does to-day. I have my serious
doubts, from what I read in my New
Testament, and from what our religion of
Jesus means, whether any one can be truly
a follower of Jesus and be what the world
calls rich. It must be given to His
suffering humanity, or we are not like
Jesus Christ; and I do not see how we
shall be able to stand face to face with
Him when He says: " I was hungry,
thirsty, naked, homeless ; what did you
do for Me?" And when we ask : "When,

Lord, did I see you thus ? " He will say :
" Inasmuch as ye did it not to one of
these, ye did it not to Me." I shall return from the East with some very solemn
convictions. If the religion of Jesus is
anything, it is a relationship of love ; and
there is great danger of our Christianity
losing its charm, and its place being taken
by church or vague sentiment, or something less than the love that makes the
soul cry out : —

> " I cannot live if Thou remove,
> For Thou art all in all ! "

Oh, whatever we lose, let us not lose
our " first love " !

You have only to come to the East to
see the fulfilment of Christ's own words,
for here are the very spots where the
churches were to which the Spirit ad-
dressed the warning word, bidding them

to take heed or the candlestick would be
removed out of its place. But they did
not take heed; they became rich and
proud, and the candlestick was removed.
Principles remain ever the same. Is there
no danger in our American Church?
Are we striving to be like the lowly
Nazarene? Do we care for the poor and
warn the rich? Are we ambitious to live
on the East Side of the city of New York,
where we are more needed, perhaps, than
on the West Side? I shall never forget
what the self-sacrificing Dr. Wheeler said
to me. We were anxious to get away
from the dirt of Jerusalem, and he said,
so sweetly, " Won't you help us to make
it clean? "

I came nearest to having what I imagined I should have, one afternoon in
returning from Bethany to Jerusalem. I
looked off on the country and said : " He

looked at these skies and these hills."
Just then Mr. Clark, who was by my
side on his donkey, said : " Undoubtedly
our Lord walked this way every afternoon
on His way to Bethany to the home of
Martha and Mary," and then I had something that will remain with me. And then
on the Mount of Olives I really seemed
to see Him as He beheld the city and
wept over it. O Jerusalem ! I am
sure if I were a Jew, the place of wailing
by the old wall would be the most natural
place for me to go.

As I have wandered among the ruins
in Jerusalem, how true to the letter the
words of Jeremiah have been fulfilled.
" The Lord hath accomplished His fury ;
He hath poured out His fierce anger, and
hath kindled a fire in Zion, and it hath
devoured the foundations thereof. The
kings of the earth, and all the inhabitants

of the world, would not have believed that
the adversary and the enemy should have
entered into the gates of Jerusalem."
The words of the Old Testament as well
as the words of the New Testament become such living words after you have
seen the land, — you exclaim so naturally,
" How is the gold become dim ! How
is the most fine gold changed ! The
stones of the sanctuary are poured out
in the top of the street. The precious
sons of Zion, comparable to fine gold,
how are they esteemed as earthen
pitchers, the work of the hands of the
potter."

It is deeply interesting as you walk
these dirty streets to think how many
Jerusalems are beneath your feet : no
less than eight are lying one upon another.
Some one has reckoned them up for us.
1st. The city of the Jebusites. 2d.

The city of Solomon. 3d. Of Nehemiah.
4th. Of Herod. 5th. The city as re-
built by Hadrian. 6th. The early Moslem
city. 7th. The Crusaders' city. 8th.
The later Moslem, which still stands
ingloriously on the wreck and ruin of all
that preceded it. Forty feet, we are told,
under the Via Dolorosa are Roman pavements over which passed the victorious
legions nearly two thousand years ago.
Jerusalem will always be sad to me; and
I was glad to go out of the city to see the
Mount of Olives and Bethany and sweet,
though mournful Gethsemane.

Dr. Wheeler, of the Medical Mission
in Jerusalem, told me — and no man has
such means of knowing as Dr. Wheeler,
he has been here so many years — that
the faith of many of the Jews is simply
sublime. They hold on to the promises made unto the fathers with a grip

that never lets go, and they say He must
fulfil His promises. All the land will
be theirs; and there is a feeling among
the Mohammedans that the land is not
theirs and their time is short. The Jews
are gathering here very fast now, — there
are three times as many Jews here now as
there were twelve years ago, — and the
soil is one of the richest in the world.
Dr. Wheeler also told me that, at the rate
of forty cents a day, you can have about
everything you want to eat. I have never
seen such cauliflowers in my life; at least
four times the size of ours, and only about
two or three cents apiece. And never
have I seen such meat displayed, — sheep
and lambs ready for the market, so white
and glistening that it was pleasant to look
at them. And as for oranges, they will
make home oranges too poor to look at.
And the grapes in the season are sold for

next to nothing; such delicious grapes, they tell me.

It seems as if there must be a future for Jerusalem, and the question will come, Does He not remember the place where He suffered and died? Only one thing has reconciled me to the fact that the followers of Mahomet have held possession of the land, — they have kept it Oriental; we are indebted to them for that. I never felt sure that any of the places pointed out to me as the exact spots where our Lord stood or suffered were where they were said to be; still we are indebted to the Armenian, Greek, and Latin churches for keeping sacred so many spots that must be near, if not on, the identical places where they assure us He stood. But I must be true and tell you there is much that is disappointing in Jerusalem. I remember an hour when I said to myself, " If I could

have gone to Samaria, and seen the well
(you feel sure of the wells) where Jesus
sat, when wearied, it seems to me I should
have been satisfied." But in that hour my
spirit seemed to hear the calm voice of the
Spirit saying, " Woman, believe me, the
hour cometh, when ye shall neither in this
mountain, nor yet at Jerusalem, worship the
Father. . . . God is a Spirit: and they
that worship Him must worship Him
in Spirit and in Truth." And in that
hour I saw how much better it would be
to have the well of water in me, than to sit
on the well and imagine Christ by my
side. It is the indwelling Christ we
need; not even the historic Christ is
enough. How deep His words were as
they came to me in Jerusalem where He
had said, " Nor yet at Jerusalem. . . .
Whosoever drinketh of the water that I
shall give him shall never thirst. The

water that I shall give him shall be in him a well of water springing up into everlasting life." Yes, that was the well I needed, and not the well at Samaria.

CAN it be possible I have seen Bethany?
Can it be I have passed over the
road where His Blessed Feet trod, day
after day, when, tired with the day's work,
He wended His way to the house of
Martha and Mary? Oh, how indebted we
come to feel towards those two women,
when we think how they made it seem
like home to Him! Some day we shall
thank them. We feel the same way towards that unknown man who put a
pillow under His head on that fishing-
boat, while He slept through the storm till
the cry of human distress awakened him
(the storm of wind and rain did not).

On my way from Bethany, I saw the
lilies of the field on either side of me; and

as I looked on the blue sky, and thought it was the very sky He looked upon, and gazed off to the hills at which David looked when he said, " I lift up mine eyes to the hills," at last I realised I was in the Holy Land; and at one spot of that road, which I seem to see now, on my way back to Jerusalem, I almost felt that I should see Him. Oh, it was so near to seeing Him! I had said so often, —

"I wish that His hands had been placed on my head,
That His arm had been thrown around me,
And that I might have seen His kind look when
He said,
Let the little ones come unto me."

And I was in the very place where He said it; and yet He said, " It is expedient for you that I go away." Oh, yes, I knew it all; but it has been expedient that so many have gone away, but once in a while the heart will cry out, " Oh, for the touch

of a vanished hand!" I really wanted to
see His face that day; but never mind,
that is ahead, for it is written, "and they
shall see His face." Ah, me — the lepers
were around me, but One who did not
fear touching them (I did) was not there.
O the Man of Galilee! The Man of
Nazareth — why did they not call Him
the Child of Bethlehem?

After Peter was baptised with the Holy
Ghost, he called Him "The holy child
Jesus." Ah, we need a supernatural power
to enable us to know a supernatural being,
and such was Jesus Christ. No one knew
that better than the early disciples did, for
they said, "No man can call Jesus, Lord,
but by the Holy Ghost."

My last look at dear, hallowed Bethany
was late one afternoon while the sun was
setting, and then, too, I had my final view
of the walled city. Shall I ever see it

again? Will it yet be in some future a glorious city? Well, I am glad there is a New Jerusalem where the gates are not shut at all, for there is no night there. To me Jerusalem the golden will have a newer meaning after this visit to old Jerusalem.

> "For thee, O dear, dear country!
>   Mine eyes their vigils keep;
> For very love, beholding
>   Thy holy name, they weep:
> The mention of thy glory
>   Is unction to the breast,
> And medicine in sickness,
>   And love, and life, and rest.

> "O sweet and blessèd country,
>   The home of God's elect!
> O sweet and blessèd country
>   That eager hearts expect!
> Jesus, in mercy bring us
>   To that dear land of rest;
> Who art, with God the Father,
>   And Spirit, ever blest."

I WAS allowed to go out much sooner than I had expected, by my physician, the good Dr. Wheeler, whom my friend secured for me as soon as we reached Jerusalem. She pleaded so hard that one of his deaconesses should come as nurse, that he consented, though she could hardly be spared from the hospital. I think if six nurses could have helped me, my friend would have had them all there. (I shall plead more feelingly for the cause of the deaconesses than I could have done had I not known the sweet ministry of Sister Margery.) And before going further, I must tell you of Dr.

Wheeler, a medical missionary, whose mission is supported by the English Church in London. The mission has a wonderful hospital in course of building, to which Dr. Wheeler is devoting all his energies. How strange it seemed that a medical missionary should come to me in my illness, when almost the last time that I spoke before sailing from New York was at our Board of Ladies of the Medical Missions. And here I was in Jerusalem, with a physician that could tell me all about the Medical Missionary work in Jerusalem; and as soon as I could talk, I was not slow in asking questions, you may be sure. I found that he was especially devoted to the poor Jews, though caring for all who came to the hospital, and trying to win the Moslems, just by loving kindness; never speaking to them of their faith, only treating them as brothers. The poor things cannot understand how the missionaries are willing to do it without receiving pay; and when they come to ask the missionaries why they do it, the opportunity comes to speak of Jesus whose religion is love.

How sure I became while in the East of the truth of the old hymn we used to sing, —

> " Love only can the conquest win,
> The strength of sin subdue."

When I spoke to Dr. Wheeler of the loss of the spirit in the worship of the letter, and the weariness to me of all the symbols, he shook his head, as he said, " You do not know this Oriental mind as I do; take these away, and you take all away from them; they have n't the Western mind; they must have the symbols."

A Sunshine Trip

I was not strong when I set out to visit
the Mount of Olives ; but Mr. Clark had
a comfortable chair for me, and I was carried by two Arabs, and Sister Margery
was on her donkey on one side of me,
and Mr. Clark on the other. It was no
little favour to have Mr. Clark ; and I love
to linger in memory on those hours at the
Mount of Olives, for I did not have
another so full of spiritual enjoyment.
Never shall I forget the moment when
the Arabs who carried me put their burden down, and Mr. Clark said, " Look
back, Mrs. Bottome." As I turned, the
city was before me, so compact with the
wall around it. None who have ever
seen that sight, felt that surprise, will ever
forget it ; and, undoubtedly, our Lord
had stood there when He looked at the
city and wept over it. The words came
back — " O Jerusalem, Jerusalem, thou

that killest the prophets, and stonest them
which are sent unto thee, how often would
I have gathered thy children together, even
as a hen gathereth her chickens under
her wings, and ye would not! Behold,
your house is left unto you *desolate.*"
One must be in Jerusalem to fully take
in the word "desolate." It is the only
word. Shall I ever forget that place of
wailing, where they press their foreheads
to the remains of the old wall of that once
beautiful city! Afterwards, when I found
myself on the top of Mount Zion and
recalled the words, " Beautiful for situ-
ation, the joy of the whole earth is Mount
Zion," I understood more fully the meaning of His words, " Behold, your house
is left unto you desolate."

It was a memorable hour to me when
I stood on the platform surrounding the
lofty minaret marking the place of the

Ascension. I was so eager to see all
the land below that I told Mr. Clark I
was quite sure I would not mind the
steep ascent up the iron stairway to the
top. How glad I was to get where there
was nothing to disturb one's thoughts!
The view from the top of this tower
is one of the finest in the world.
Walking around the balcony, it seemed
as if the whole land were close to me.
And it was not difficult to imagine that
little group, with Jesus in the midst of
them, coming along the road to the spot
where He would bless them, and in the
act of blessing be parted from them.

Only Mr. Clark and Sister Margery
were with me; the almost ever-present
beggars were not there. Mr. Clark knew
the land, and is a Biblical scholar, and to
be with him there was to have the "land
and the book."

I would not wish to put myself under
the care of any company but that of
Mr. Clark; and we meant it when we
said to him, on parting at Jaffa, " Refer
any party who is thinking of visiting
Palestine, or any of the countries we
have visited, to us, and we will give you
the strongest of testimonials." I look
back to that hour on the top of the
minaret as almost the only hour when
I was not in the presence of a crowd of
unfortunate beggars, clamouring for backsheesh. I heard that we should be over-
run with beggars; but I could not have
imagined the wretchedness as it actu-
ally exists, and to give was only to in-
crease the crowd. Not a sacred spot,
scarcely, could you see but in the presence of the Mohammedans. The sun
was setting as I was carried down the
hill, ashamed of being carried where

He walked; and there seemed a peculiar meaning in the lines that came to my mind: —

" I blush in all things to abound, the servant is above his Lord." The lilies of the field, the same He looked at when He said, " Behold the lilies ! " were on either side of me — " Solomon, in all his glory, was not arrayed like one of these." The lilies are of the brightest scarlet hue; and I was told that the shade could not be obtained by dyes in Solomon's time. It was literally true, therefore, that Solomon, in all his glory, could not match that beautiful shade of colour. I saw the Mount of Olives and the beautiful lilies for the last time that afternoon. But love never forgets, its past is ever present, its yesterday is always to-day. Love makes every memory say, " Lo, I am with you alway,

even unto the end of the world." And
so I join my prayer with another, " Let
Thy love make the past a present to me,
let it bring to the gates of my life the
footsteps of the Son of man, let it make
my country a Palestine, *my* family-circle
a Bethany, *my* cross a Calvary, and *my*
crown an Olivet ! "

A GARDEN where an old monk gives you flowers, and where you see old olive trees; where you wish the old monk would go away and leave you there alone; where you would like to sit under the olive trees in the twilight and then— Ah! " The light of the world cannot reveal the glories of Gethsemane. It can disclose the sweat-drops and the tears and the darkness. It can reveal the suppliant pouring forth His petition with the voice of strong crying. It can show that the prayer is seemingly unanswered, and the passing of the cup denied; but cannot disclose the peace that comes with the cup.

It cannot detect the angel of strength
that follows the surrendered will."

O Gethsemane, what should we do
without thee? " Not my will, but Thine
be done." You see (if you have eyes
to see) while there, that every rose and
flower that is handed you, or that you
may take, you owe all to His agony in
that garden. It is fitting it should be
a garden. We owe all our gardens, inside and outside, to the love that only
" feared " that His strength might not
hold out till His work for us should be
finished on the cross. He was heard
in that He feared, and there was an
angel sent to strengthen Him. Surely,
we can say of Gethsemane, as we say
of Calvary, " Thou art Heaven on
earth to me, lovely, mournful Calvary."
When we think of what His " Thy
will be done " has been to the saints

for nearly two thousand years, as they
have entered their Gethsemane, — and all,
sooner or later, have had their Gethsemane, — you can hear the echo of
His " Thy will be done " in their

" Thy will, not mine, O Lord,
However hard it be ; "

and every note of that song we owe to
His " Thy will be done." Oh, what an
opportunity those three disciples lost !
Why did they go to sleep ? All their
after cowardice might not have been if they
had not lost that opportunity. Maybe
it is because we do not draw near to the
suffering Son of God, and enter into the
fellowship of His sufferings, that this suffering world is allowed to bear its agony.
We indulge ourselves, instead of being
like the angel that strengthened Him.
Farewell ! sad, but beautiful Gethsemane !

"O LITTLE town of Bethlehem."
All I saw of Bethlehem that I
shall love to remember was what I saw
with my spirit eyes the morning I lay in
my bed at the Howard Hotel in Jerusalem,
when my nurse, who was at the window
in the early morning, said, " Oh, Mrs.
Bottome, I wish you could see the view
from this window ; here is the road that
leads to Bethlehem." I closed my eyes,
and I saw the road that leads *from* Bethlehem, thronged with happy children, every
one of them knowing that Jesus said,
" Suffer the little children to come unto
me. . . . And He took them up in His
arms, put His hands upon them and blessed

them." Oh, that road *from* Bethlehem! The joy of the world comes direct from Bethlehem. " Jesus was born in Bethlehem." The angels sang there ; and there the Wise Men brought their presents. O Spirit of God, preserve from fading the dayspring from on high! let the Spirit preserve from setting the star that rose in Bethlehem. We need the Spirit to quicken our memories.

In the Holy Land, and especially in Bethlehem, did His words come with such force into my heart, " *The Kingdom is within you.*" My disappointment in Bethlehem was complete. It was the only rainy day we had while on the trip ; and yet we had the sunrise when my nurse stood at the window in the early morning, and, if I remember correctly, the rain ceased in the late afternoon; but I went to and returned from Bethlehem in a pouring rain.

I went to the Church of the Nativity, where you see the manger. There are two altars, one for the Greek Church and the other for the Latin Church. One church owns the manger, and the other the silver star, over which is an altar. Standing guard over these two representative Christian churches are the armed Turkish soldiers, to keep these Christians from killing one another!

They hate each other so, with a perfect hatred; and that was Bethlehem! I wanted to get away, as I did so many other times, for the spirit was lost in the letter. Over the manger hang gold and silver lamps; indeed, here, as in the Church of the Holy Sepulchre, the silver and gold were everywhere; but your very heart cried out: "Where is the Christ, the Incarnate Son of God, whose name is Love?"

The rain was so great that I could only glance at Rachel's tomb. All venerate her, Mohammedans, Jews, and Christians. Poor old Jacob! If it had been a clear day, and I had had time (alas! that commodity was so scarce), I should have liked to dream a little while of the past at her grave. "Call the child Ben-oni!" There was one thing about her tomb, — you felt sure of it; and that was more than you could say of many other places.

Of course, you are expected to stay and see the well; and they told me the water was delicious; David liked it. There was also a fascination for me in the cave of Adullam. But perhaps I had expected too much from seeing Bethlehem. Anyway, I shall have no pleasant, holy remembrance of it. It eases my mind to make this confession.

The Church of the Nativity is almost a horror to me. I have a great admiration for the Empress Helena. When I saw her statue afterwards in Rome, I greeted it as an old friend; but I never could imagine anything more hollow than the services in the Nativity Church. As for the choir boys, gazing around and turning to look at us, and the selling of the wax tapers, I should have thought a scourge of small cords not out of place just then. As Bethlehem is now, the words, " Let us now go even unto Bethlehem," would have no attractive power for me.

THIS mosque surrounds a rugged piece of rock. To the Mohammedan this is the most holy place in the world, next to Mahomet's tomb. From this rock you are told Mahomet ascended to heaven. I looked at the rock that tried to follow. They told us the angel Gabriel came down and held it till Mahomet got clear; they show you the finger-marks of Gabriel, for he had all he could do to hold the rock down. The reason why this spot is so sacred to the Jew is that he believes this rock to be the Moriah on which Abraham offered up Isaac, — the actual spot where the sacred Ark rested.

We did not go down into the cave —
or at least I did not. Perhaps you remember that General Gordon begged to
be allowed to open the hole in the floor.
I have read that he was refused. They
believe it to be the entrance into the
lower world. Gordon, however, thought
otherwise, and after excavating in the
Kedron Valley he came on some conduit
which apparently ran right up to this
rock. He at once concluded that this
opening in the rock was to carry off the
blood and water of the sacrifices in old
time. It is fully believed that on this
rock stood the great brazen altar.

Underneath this mosque you are told
that Solomon stabled his horses; and
these stables are known as Solomon's.
Two thousand horses can be cared for
here.

There is a walled-up gate that is very

interesting. It is called "The Golden Gate." The Mohammedans have a legend concerning it. The tradition is that the conquerors of Zion will enter through this gate, and the power in Jerusalem will pass from the Moslem to the Jews. Therefore the gate is walled up that entrance may be impossible.

The Jew believes the tradition, and quietly waits for the time when the Golden Gate shall be thrown open for the Messiah to enter and reign over His people. I hope it may be, but I wish they would open their hearts to Him now. Yet I cannot help thinking He loves the city where He worked and suffered and died; and here, as in other places, especially on the Mount of Olives, it does seem to me He will yet stand, and the feet marked with the print of the nails will yet press this soil.

IT is not always best to speak or write of what we have missed in life; it is so much better to dwell on what we have not missed. But I must tell you, because you will ask me, what I missed particularly. First, Nazareth, where " He was brought up," and where I had so much anticipated going. For it had seemed to me the beautiful scene in our New Testament would be more precious still, if I could have imagined His voice on the very spot (if that could be) where He stood up and read the prophecy concerning Himself — " The Spirit of the Lord is upon me, because He hath anointed me to preach the Gospel to the poor; to

bind up the broken-hearted . . . to set at
liberty them that are bruised, to preach the
acceptable year of the Lord." But I did
not see Nazareth. Now what can I do,
having missed it? Well, it seems to me
I must use my imagination, and in spirit
listen to the words that can never grow
old, because always needed. And this
may be a comfort to some of you who
will never visit the Holy Land.

Then, I also missed the Sea of Galilee.
This was a still greater loss to me, for I
had dreamed of sitting by the sea, or the
lake, and looking at the same kind of
boats in which He so often sat, and the
fishing smacks, those which one sees to-
day. He had said such wonderful things;
but missing it has taught me we might
associate Him with every sea and every
lake if we only would; for all lakes and
rivers and seas are His, and we might so

often see His form on the sea in imagination. It has been said, "Faith has still its
Olivet, and love its Galilee," and, as I
write, one place after another comes up
that I had so fully expected to see, but
missed.

I did not see the Damascus road, where
a light above the brightness of the sun
shone on Saint Paul and he heard the
words, " Saul, Saul, why persecutest
thou me?" Ah, he never forgot those
words, *I am Jesus.* I do not know
how intensified the story would have been
if I had gone to Damascus, but I know
that I have, since I returned, read all
these incidents in my New Testament
with increasing interest; and yet I must
be honest and say that in spiritual travel,
— spiritual light that illuminates the truths
of our Bibles to us can only come in com-
panionship with the Holy Spirit, — we

may stand on the most sacred spots in
the world, and all be common soil to us;
but with the Spirit in us, whether we step
on the Holy Land or not, all will be holy
ground to us. No one knows better than
I do to-day how much or how little all
these sacred places may be to us: "We
perceive as we are."

And yet I can confess to the disappointment in missing the overland trip; though
now I can see how unwise it would have
been to have attempted it when the
Bedouin tribes were so restless, and there
was such a spirit of uneasiness through all
the East. For though these Bedouin
tribes claim to be direct descendants of
Abraham, they are natural born robbers,
and it is always unsafe for any one to pass
through their country unguarded; and
though mounted Turkish soldiers were to
be our escort, we did not feel by any

means sure of them. "Turkish soldiers" had not a very restful sound to us. We knew these Bedouin tribes were after money; for the head of each tribe is legally required to pay the Sultan one Turkish pound, nearly five dollars, a year. In this way only can they be exempt from military duty. Early in May, near the time we expected to be there, a party was visiting the Jordan and Dead Sea with the usual guard. Four of the number separated from the others; and in less than two hours they were seized, robbed of their horses, money, and clothing, and a most pitiable lot they were when they reached their tents after nightfall.

We valued our lives too highly to take the risk of the tent life that had appeared so fascinating to us in anticipation. So, when disappointed, I feel I must do as I have done so many

times in my life, — organise victory out
of defeat. But the hardest part was
to have to disappoint others. When I
thought of the King's Daughters who
wrote me from Smyrna, saying, "We
are so sad here in the East, and we feel
your coming will give us hope," and
when I thought of the two hundred
young girls who were to have a holiday
when I should arrive at Beyroot, the disappointment was keener still.

Yet I said to myself, surely He is guid-
ing me. Did I not ask for guidance; did
I not say as one of old said, in the very
land I had gone to see, "If Thy presence
go not with me, carry me not up hence"?
Often God has purposes to work out
through our disappointments that are too
deep for us to see at the time, and I could
not forget that all that others had received
from me in the past that had been of any

benefit to them had come from my poverty,
never from my riches; so I said, it may
be that others will in some way be en-
riched by what I have missed, rather than
by what I had hoped to have. Any way,
the blessed "all things" remain, and the
"all things" take in what we have missed.

Of course, I determined to make the
most of what remained, and what you do
see in the Holy Land somehow never
leaves you. It is a long way to the Orient,
but I would not hesitate to go again, if
my Guide led me there. And indeed
what an education it is to have such a
courier with you, as we had in Mr. Valentine, and how we vexed him by staying
so short a time in each place! He felt all
the time what we were missing; he knew
everything, and was ready to tell us what
we did not know: and his soul was vexed;
I could see it from day to day. But his

business was to take care of us, to guide us, and he did it well. He illustrated the sweet words, "He careth for you." He did not want us to look after anything, not even our wraps, or our little hand-bags. When we entered a car, we were sure to find everything safely put up above us or at our side. How proud he was of "the boy" of our party! He felt he owned us all. To be sure, it took us a little time to get used to being owned; but where would we have been without him? He knew all the languages we did not know; and before we were through, we found he was the man of consequence, for the best hotels knew him. I am sure, if I should take the trip again, I should look out for Mr. Clark and the courier, Mr. Valentine, he provided for us.

And now the question is, Shall I take in the lesson that I have a Guide — one who

wishes to take care of everything for me —
who is constantly preparing places for me
so that I always go into a prepared place?
To realise this always would be worth a
trip to the Orient.

I HAVE just read a letter sent to one of our party from Mr. R——, who left us at Jaffa to visit Constantinople and Athens. Both were in our itinerary, but the distance by boat between Jaffa and Constantinople was so great, and the younger ones of our party were so tired of boats, and as the East had not been so fascinating to them as to us older ones, and they were eager to reach the Continent, we took our steamer for Brindisi. Mr. R. writes from Beyroot. "When I arrived at the American (Presbyterian) Mission I was more than pleased. The grounds are beautifully laid out, the buildings are splendid, and the stone

church is the best I have seen in the
East. They have four hundred pupils
of both sexes. Dr. and Mrs. Bliss, the
heads of the institution, have lived here
forty years. The Doctor was absent, but
we saw the charming Mrs. Bliss in her
beautiful home. They have been wonderfully successful in establishing a grand
work. Mr. William E. Dodge and Mr.
Morris K. Jesup, of New York, are two
of the principal trustees and contributors.
Another Mr. Jesup is our American
Minister, or Consul General, here. They
were all disappointed when I told them
that Mrs. Bottome had gone back via
Alexandria, and would not visit them.
They had been expecting her ; and Mr.
Jesup had promised the two hundred
young ladies in the school a half holiday
when Mrs. Bottome arrived, and they
were to have had an afternoon tea, and

to have given her a reception. They had no idea that she had been quarantined in their harbour."

I am not apt to take so much space telling what I have missed; but I want these dear friends who are passing through so much trial in that disturbed land to know that I would have made every effort in my power to have reached them, if I had known two hundred dear girls were looking for me. While quarantined at Beyroot, I did think of the institution, and of the noble work they were doing, and said to myself how sorry Mrs. William E. Dodge will be when I return and tell her I did not see the institution to which she has been, and to which she is, so devoted. "What I missed" is very suggestive. We are always missing something, because life is made up of choices. We must leave something to have any-

thing; and we often, I fear, leave something for that which proves to be less than
nothing. How much we need wisdom,
how much we should ask for it, that we
may not miss the most important things!

O N our return from Jerusalem to Jaffa, waiting for the Austrian steamer to take us to Port Said, I remembered that our Greek dragoman had spoken of an English school in Jaffa, so I asked him where I should find it. As I intended taking a donkey ride, he offered to walk beside me and show me. We went through the town, finding it more crowded than ever, as it was a feastday, — the long fast of the Ramazan had just ended. I remembered being in a mosque in Cairo when Lent commenced. All is gaiety now; the women and little girls have on their best gowns, and all look happy. As we entered the gate leading to the large stone house, I noticed a white marble slab in the wall at the side of the door, and on it the words, Isaiah liv. 10. The history of it was given me just before leaving.

I was ushered into the school by one of the teachers, a lovely-looking girl, who took me into a room where the larger girls were. They all stood while I said a few words to them ; they were exceedingly bright-looking, and were a mixture of Jewesses, Moslems, and Christians. After speaking to the different classes in different rooms, Miss Walker-Arnott, the founder of this school, and the one who has carried on the Tabitha Mission in Jaffa, introduced herself to me, and took me into the drawing-room for a little chat. It was then I learned that she had come here alone to Jaffa, and had built

this large house with her private fortune.
She was under no society, and had not
had a commission till of late years. The
children she gathered around her then,
are her teachers now; and it was her am-
bition to educate, and then have them in
turn educate others. I learned that there
were a Home, or boarding-school; three
schools in town; a Sunday-School in the
Home, for scholars from the three town
schools; a meeting for women in the
town; a class meeting for men in the
Home; and a Bible woman visiting in
the town.

There are a number of native assist-
ants, trained in the Institution, and on
the roll are the names of one hundred and
seventy children of different faiths; but
I noticed this morning when I repeated the
words of Jesus, " Suffer the little children
to come unto Me," they all repeated it

with me. Miss Arnott told me that the
work among the Moslem women had
been particularly encouraging. The children were taught to think and judge and
act, and are incited to pass that highest
standard which is such a purely Western
importation in the East, namely, faithful-
ness and veracity. A sweet spirit per-
vaded the house, a something that made
you think it might be Bethany, where
Jesus would be sure to come. I was so
glad she gave me the history of the
marble plate in the wall. She said that
after the wall was completed and the
foundations all securely laid, persecution
began. One day she was nearly worn
out; she seemed on the edge of completely breaking down; and at last felt
so discouraged that she laid down on a
lounge and realised that all the energy,
strength, and enthusiasm that had kept

her going had really left her. She had
laid her fortune and life down, and had
not accomplished the work she had under-
taken to do. Just at that moment one of
her trusty workmen came in and asked
her if she knew who had written on the
wall outside. She asked what was written,
and the answer was just this: Isaiah
liv. 10. She opened her Bible and read:
" For the mountains shall depart, and the
hills be removed ; but My kindness shall
not depart from thee, neither shall the
covenant of My peace be removed, saith
the Lord that hath mercy on thee."

She told me that when she read it, new
strength came to her, she rose from the
lounge and was well again. So she kept
the words that were written with charcoal on the stone as long as she could,
then had them cut in a plate. She never
knew who wrote them, but imagined

that some travellers had pitched their tents
in the night, and seeing this unfinished
building, just wrote the text with a bit of
charcoal. The work they did they never
knew.

I really needed to get a glimpse of
something real, and am glad I have the
picture of the Tabitha School to hang up
on the walls of memory. I have been so
sick of the sights and sounds that have
greeted me in the past in the Holy Land.
Oh, to have sat down by the Lake of
Galilee; and yet, knowing as I do, how
unlike it is to what you imagined it would
be, it is far better to be with Him on
every lake in spirit. That, perhaps, is
the reason He said, " It is expedient for
you that I go away," then " I will be
with you always and everywhere." Oh,
yes, *He* is our Holy Land! The Promised Land! Life itself is only a symbol,

a figure of the true. So I will take up the little refrain that has helped me so much.

" Where He may lead I'll follow,
My trust in Him repose,
And every hour in perfect peace,
I'll sing He knows!"

ON the morning of the 24th of March we stepped from our steamer (which we took at Alexandria) on to the continent of Europe at Brindisi. How many times at important events of my life the word has come with a new force: "I beseech you, by the mercies of God, that ye present your bodies a living sacrifice"! And I felt that morning that the old hymn of my childhood was the appropriate one for me, —

"Thy ransomed servant, I
Restore to Thee thine own,
And from this moment live or die,
To serve my God alone."

It took us all day to reach Naples. As we approached the city I saw the fires from Mount Vesuvius. I must confess I did not feel as if I wished to go very near them. Until very recently Cook's Cable Railway has been very convenient for those who have wished to go to the top; but of late the eruptions have been uncommonly frequent, and the road completely blocked by the lava. It is now a very toilsome trip, if not a dangerous one, and I learned a lesson on the Nile I do not intend to forget. I took risks in the excessive heat that I would not take again, so I decided to content myself with "looking up" without going up. Naples has interested me exceedingly. I find it a much larger city than I had anticipated. It is considered the most beautifully situated city in Europe. The bay is a dream of beauty; one American enthusiast said, "See Naples and die." I should rather say, "After seeing it, what must the pure river of water of life be?" Earth is so shadowed. The first thing I heard this morning was a band of music, and, looking out of my window, I saw the fresh troops marching to the scene of war. Three thousand left yesterday. As I thought of all the sorrow of so many mothers at parting with their sons, never to see them, perhaps, again, the lines of Mrs. Browning came so forcibly to my mind, —

"Dead! . . .
  Both! both my boys! If . . .
    You want a great song for your Italy free,
      Let none look at *me !*"

The contrasts here, as everywhere, are so sharp between great poverty and extreme riches! The horses are uncommonly fine. I think I never saw so many beautiful horses in so short a space of time as I saw on the afternoon we

drove around the city; but the faces of
the poor are pathetic, and their press-
ing cry for help meets you everywhere.
It does seem as if when you get where
nature is the most beautiful, man is in
the extremest need. What will it be to
see a city, "so holy and clean no sorrow
can breathe in the air"! When poverty
and filth was on every side of me in
Jerusalem, how much to me was the
anticipation of "Jerusalem the golden"!
It is not here.

We were relieved on entering Naples
not to hear the wild voices in Arabic; and
the absence of the Mohammedan loose
dress was a comfort. But, alas, we did
not escape sights and sounds that made
us shut our eyes! We have been enabled to do much more than we possibly
could have done through all the trip by
riding instead of walking. Nothing sur-

prises an Italian more than people walking when they could ride; they detest
walking. I certainly have an affinity with
them in that respect. After all, we are
the same people travelling that we are at
home.

It was a source of much amusement
that I took a nap one afternoon in a tomb.
I am more indebted to that nap, perhaps,
than I shall ever know. We had been
exploring the tombs at Thebes, and having
ridden many miles on our donkeys, we
were not aware how hot the sun was.
When we came out of the tomb, just at
the entrance, where we were sheltered, our
dragoman had spread a rug, and had prepared for us a very nice lunch. When
luncheon was finished, and dishes and
cloth were removed, the rug looked so
tempting that I threw myself down and
slept three quarters of an hour, I am

told. That sleep saved me, for I was the only one that did not succumb to the heat on the return to the boat. So I was very glad I did take my usual nap, although in a tomb.

A MONG the fascinating novels of my girlhood was " The Last Days of Pompeii," and so I was all ready for the trip to Pompeii our second day in Naples. We started early in the morning, and found, when we reached the railway station, that there had been a change in the time-table since the day before, and our train had gone. There was nothing to do but to take carriages ; but we anticipated a delightful ride over a country road, and supposed we should be in sight of the beautiful bay. Well, we did n't have what we expected ; but that is not an uncommon thing in life. We took the long ride over the stony pavements all the way to Pompeii. We did see new sights; we saw more macaroni than we shall ever see again, hanging like curtains on the sidewalk, and we certainly saw enough faded glory to last us a long time. You could see that all the houses of the poor had once been dwellings of the wealthy; and not a house, scarcely, without a balcony at every window! Most of them were in different shades of the colours so peculiar to Naples, — a salmon pink, or white, or dark brown, — and on many of the houses were faded paintings.

I was pleasantly disappointed in the ruins. The wall decorations lend a peculiar charm. The lower part of the colums are covered with painted stucco. The colours I was not prepared for, and they were very pleasant to see. The red and yellow seem appropriate in this brilliant Southern sun. Of course the best of everything that has been discovered has been taken to the remarkable Museum in Naples.

As I was carried through what was once a theatre, the House of Commerce, temples and colonnades, I had a good opportunity to reflect and learn lessons that I fear I should not have learned if I had been tired by walking. It seemed so wonderful that this was the ancient city mentioned in history three hundred and ten years before Christ, and which fifty-nine years after the birth of Christ was the favourite resort of the wealthier class. In the year 63, Mount Vesuvius, which had been quiet for centuries, became active, and a great earthquake destroyed a good part of the beautiful city. But they went right to work, rebuilding in the Roman style, and when the final catastrophe occurred in 79, much was unfinished. I looked at a row of columns that were in

course of building when all was buried;
and of all the wonders of excavation I
have seen in this trip, in some respects
this seemed the most wonderful. To
think that all remained completely buried
for fifteen centuries! and we saw the marvellous statuary in the Museum at Naples,
and the bronzes that are the wonder of the
world! One of our party, Mrs. G——,
was particularly anxious to see the kitchen
utensils that had been unearthed, and when
one thinks that Pompeii represents almost
the only source of our acquaintance with
ancient and domestic life, we have a
right to be interested in the kitchen utensils. Excavations! There is a peculiar
charm in the word to me; buried treasures! Much is buried. I think I shall
sing the old song with a new meaning,—

" Touched by a human heart,
Wakened by kindness,

174

Pompeii

Chords that were broken
Will vibrate once more."

It might help us in our work to think
that every kind word and kind act is help-
ing to remove the rubbish that encases
the lost image. I remember standing
and watching, while in a tomb in Egypt,
as the soil was removed; and all at once
a treasure was in sight. Passing along,
you could see here and there images peep-
ing out of the great wall, — valuable discoveries that had just been made, — and
nothing I had ever seen was like these
buried treasures that had at last come to
light. Oh, if we could take courage when
working, *excavating*, trying to find the
buried soul, and when at last the tear
starts, feel that the treasure is in view!
The soul is there!

Again and again, while in the East, I
thought of our own dreadful East Side,

where there is so much of want. Thank
God for those who are willing to do the
work of excavating ! Some day a great
joy will come to those who look on the
beautiful soul, — not a statue in a museum,
but a beautiful spirit in the Father's
house. Will not the joy pay for all the
toil, as memory takes them back to the
days when they were engaged in the work
of unearthing, bringing to light and joy,
God's buried treasures ?

CANON FARRAR says it was the dream of Saint Paul's life to preach Christ in Rome, then the centre of civilisation; but if he had had his dream fulfilled, we might not have had his " letters from Rome." It is an interesting study, to say the least, to think how much poorer this world would be to-day if some people had had that of which they dreamed and for which they longed. Think of what an inspiration the world would have lost if it could not have had imagined that noblest of men sitting in his hired house chained to a Roman soldier, writing letters that will live in character long after all that made Rome the imperial city shall have crumbled into dust! How much greater is Saint Paul than Rome! This thought never left me while sight-seeing in what is called (but is not) " the eternal city."

The two great objects of interest to me, and those which I had wanted to see from a child, were St. Peter's Church and the Colosseum. If I had stayed a month in Rome, I should have wanted to visit St. Peter's every day, — the grandest edifice ever built by man, painted against God's loveliest sky, as Hawthorne speaks of it. The approach to the cathedral is the piazza of St. Peter's, which is partly surrounded by curved colonnades. In the centre of the piazza is the great obelisk brought from the Egyptian Heliopolis. I have read that during the erection of this monument, in 1586, the engineer neglected to calculate on the stretching of the ropes, and the great shaft hung sus-

pended in the air, and because of the strain
on the ropes it could not be placed in
position, until a sailor workman shouted,
" Pour water on the ropes." His suggestion was promptly acted upon, and the
five hundred tons of rock came safely into
place. The sailor was not punished by
the death promised to the first of the eight
hundred workmen who should speak at
that critical moment, but was rewarded
with the privilege of furnishing the palm
branches for St. Peter's on Palm Sunday.

I was not disappointed in St. Peter's,
though it was so unlike what I had expected. There is no "dim religious light"
there. The interior is very light, the
windows being of plain glass. Many magnificent marble columns that were taken
from the pagan temples stand about the
thirty beautiful altars and the monuments
in the church. Of course I stood by the

famous iron statue of Saint Peter. The great toe of this statue is indeed being worn away by the constant kissing. Our courier stood by my side, and of course kissed the bronze toe, and I saw that he noticed I did not, so I said to him, " I too love Saint Peter, and while standing here I have offered a little prayer that I might have the love he had when Jesus said to him, 'Feed my lambs.'" In that moment I thought of the many lambs that need the affection that the faithful seem to give to Saint Peter. I should have been very glad to see the Pope, and if he had not been so feeble, we probably should have been granted an interview, or, as we were in the church on Palm Sunday, we might have seen him there; but he was extremely feeble at that time.

You have read better descriptions of the wonderful church than I can give you.

I could write a book on what I saw, and did not see, in St. Peter's and the Vatican, and yet, strangely, what remains most vividly before my mind is what *you* might not have noticed. In one of the many chapels in the church there was a service on the day before Palm Sunday, where we saw a number of cardinals, and where the service was very imposing. But nothing impressed me like the figure of a woman in deep mourning as she knelt by one of the pillars. The whole service was in a language I could not understand. All the rich colours of the robes of the priests and cardinals, all the odour of the incense from swinging censers, faded from my senses as I gazed on that woman who was a figure, a symbol, to me of the broken hearts of all womankind. She never moved during the time we were in that chapel, and I seemed to see only that

woman and the unseen man of Nazareth,
who said, " He hath sent me to bind up
the broken-hearted." Oh, how my soul
turned away in that hour from everything
to the personal Christ, who can be revealed
to us only by the Holy Spirit!

I *need* to see the things that are not
seen, for they only are eternal. I have felt
this all the time I have been sight-seeing,
and if I had not come for instruction, I
should have found, as many who travel for
mere pleasure find, that it is a weariness to
the flesh, and they wish they were at home.
I heard a young girl once say : " I think
this is unendurable, this monotonous life
on the sea day after day, unless one is in
love"; and I quite agreed with her, but
I felt like singing, " Jesus, lover of my
soul." Oh, what a difference companion-
ship makes, what a difference it has made
to me ! How much more the wonders of

art have been to me after praying, "Show me what You want me to see, and let me see the meaning of things, not the mere things"!

It seems to me one cannot but be impressed here in Rome that it is suffering love which is crowned. Saint Peter and Saint Paul were martyrs ; they lived and they died for the good of others ; and that is the reason they are living in stone, living in the heart of humanity to-day. The cross, the symbol of this self-sacrifice, is everywhere. You are shown the very chain — the rude iron chain — they bound Saint Peter with. It is *now* in a golden case. Strange, is n't it, that many who call themselves Christians can see the symbol of the cross everywhere and not say, —

> "Must Jesus bear the cross alone,
> And all the world go free?"

But He only knows how many are bearing

the cross He has laid upon them. Saint
Peter's chains are on exhibition, but who
can tell what chains are worn by the saints
that earth does not recognise. Poverty
is a chain. I shrink from mentioning
other chains so many are wearing to-day;
but He knows His martyrs in every age.

I saw, while standing within the walls of
the great Colosseum, what I saw among the
ruins of Pompeii, and in the tombs of
the kings on the Nile, that there comes
an end to all human greatness. "Pride
goeth before destruction, and a haughty
spirit before a fall." I learned this by
heart when I was a girl, and history, the
history of nations, the history of individ-
uals, proves the truth of the saying my
mother repeated to me so often, "*Pride
will have a fall.*" Ruins! Ruins! A
great part of this trip has been made up
of seeing ruins. A gentleman well known

in New York City said to me the other
day, "What a pity that theological stu-
dents could not go to Jerusalem to finish
their studies and see the followers of the
different religions of the world before they
are let loose upon the people to preach ! "
I replied, "There is just such a theological school now being built by a very
wealthy Englishman in Jerusalem." I
would add that it is a pity that every
preacher of righteousness could not make
the trip I have made to *see*, not merely
read, the truth that " *God only is great.*"

How poor pride looked compared with
humility, when in the city of Rome I
thought of Nero and Paul and compared
the two characters ! How grand Moses
looked in Egypt compared with Rameses
the Great ! How glad he is now that he
chose rather " to suffer affliction with the
people of God than to enjoy the pleasures

of sin for a season," and the season so
short! The body, or mummy, of Rameses
the Second is on exhibition in the Museum
of Cairo, but not the body of Moses. The
last sight we caught of his body was on
the Mount of Transfiguration. A glorious body! Oh, yes, righteousness pays in
every age. I looked at the marble statue
of Moses and Michael Angelo here in
Rome a few days ago, and did not wonder
the artist struck it with a hammer after he
finished it, and said, "Why don't you
speak?" Ah, Moses had spoken, and
that was the reason he had become the
dream of poets and artists. There are
some people that have n't life enough in
them while living to ever breathe in marble after they are gone. Moses led the
children of Israel out of the land of bond-
age ; he was God's servant, and so never
died.

Thank God, we have some leaders to-
day, though not many, who are willing,
after being learned in all the art of the
schools and having prospects like Moses
had, to turn their backs on all, and instead
lead a life of utter self-effacement. The
cross is everywhere, but not the spirit of
it. And yet I am sure that He who looks
at the heart knows the lives of many
whose names will not be heralded on earth,
but who are marked with the cross and
who know the meaning of Saint Paul's
words: " I am crucified with Christ:
nevertheless, I live; . . . and the life that
I now live in the flesh, I live by the faith
of the Son of God, who loved me, and
gave Himself for me."

All the weary travel to reach *this* Mecca
will more than pay, if we reach Him who
is the real Mecca, for we can stay with
Him, and do not have to turn back to

go over the dusty road again, as I saw so many pilgrims do. When Christ is reached, there is a sense in which our travelling days are o'er : —

> " God is our home, and in that state
> We cannot so far separate
> As not to make the distant near
> And know the loved are always here."

THIS is a ruin you could never tire of seeing. Think of eighty-seven thousand spectators being accommodated on the marble seats, and fifteen thousand more who could stand and witness the games ! We looked at the four tiers of seats and imagined the first tier occupied by the Emperor, the senators, and the rest of the *élite*, including the vestal virgins. The second tier was reserved for the knights and nobles. Then came room for the plebeians. The top gallery, we are told, was used by the sailors employed in the manipulation of the immense awning that shaded the spectators and the men employed in showering perfumed water on those beneath. Think of the dedication of the Colosseum being celebrated with games which lasted one hundred days, and during which time ten thousand men and five thousand wild beasts were slain on its arena; and we stood and looked down on that arena! I thought of the thousands and thousands of Christians who perished there. I must say that the painful association that was so connected with that ruin of the most wonderful edifice ever erected took from me the enjoyment I would otherwise have had.

I did not see it by moonlight. That would be a sight! But we had been cautioned not to visit it at night unless we wanted to risk getting malaria; and we were not sentimental enough to run any risk. I had known of friends who had never recovered from the effects of dis-

ease they had taken at Rome; and all
through our trip we had been exceedingly careful. I did not forget what a
friend of mine said to me just before
leaving. In speaking of a friend who
travelled with her in the East, she said
she has never been the same woman phys-
ically since her trip to the East. We
wanted to return well, and so we did very
little at night during the entire trip.
We are told that this wonderful Colosseum, now in ruins, did not fall with
decay. Had it been left untouched by
the bandits, who ruined so many of
Rome's greatest monuments, it would
have remained intact probably to this
day. It was regarded as a sort of mine,
or quarry, from which was taken the
material to build the palaces and the
smaller buildings. One half of the only
wall is gone, and but two thirds of the

original Colosseum remains. You can form an idea of its size by the value of the material yet standing, since, as shown by a noted architect, the mere stone, brick, and marble in the ruins are worth $1,250,000. One can see the underground passage and cells in which were kept the condemned victims of the arena, both man and beast. Alas, for the human nature that could enjoy the sight of the flowing blood! To me, it is simply savage human nature. Thank God, a better day has dawned! Nothing shows more conclusively to me the fact that man is only a ruin of the image that God made him, than all that is suggested by a visit to the Colosseum at Rome.

BEAUTIFUL Venice! There is no
city like it. To float in a gondola on a moonlight night, and listen
to the music, is an experience not to be
forgotten. Now I am back in Venice
and on the Grand Canal, and looking at
the old palaces on either side that have
such a fascination for me. "The canal
is like an 'S' in shape, and cuts the city
in two nearly equal parts. It is two
miles long and about one hundred and
eighty feet wide, except at the narrow-
est places, where the famous Rialto
crosses it. This bridge of perhaps one
hundred feet span was built in 1588–
1591. It is one graceful arch of Italian

marble, on which are twenty-four shops, and three passage-ways for pedestrians. There are but three other bridges over this canal, and they are of iron. The great building of Venice is St. Mark's Cathedral, — some one calls it the 'Golden Cavern'; it is incrusted with precious stones, at once splendid and sombre, sparkling and mysterious. It is the richest cathedral in its adornments in the world. It is a partial copy of St. Sofia in Constantinople, golden-roofed, with great marble statues outlined against the five domes of the church. The sun from this consummation of the sublime in Oriental and Venetian architecture brings out the most exquisite colouring, and when the sky is glowing (as it can only glow in Venice) the effect is magnificent. Above the central portal are the four gilded horses that in 1204 were brought

from Constantinople. Napoleon stole
them, and they were taken to Paris
in 1797, as trophies of war. The
horses were returned in 1815, and
now grace the portal as of old. The
interior of the old church is as wonderful as the exterior. More than five
hundred valuable columns of precious
substances are in and about St. Mark's;
and forty-six thousand square feet of
beautiful mosaic, much of it executed in
the eleventh century, cover its floors,
walls, and ceiling." I would like to tell
you more of this wonderful cathedral;
it is so beautiful. Every one has heard
of the pigeons of St. Mark's that
swarm in this square and have been
fed by the city for seven hundred
years. "Our Henry" had a good time
feeding the pigeons, and so had the
pigeons in being fed; but they were in

great danger of being killed with kindness at his hands; he never tired feeding them. I do not like to stop writing of the weird old city. I did not go again to the palace of the Doges, or over the Bridge of Sighs, or down through the dreadful dungeons that I was so determined to explore a few months before, but I left Venice saying, as I think every one says, " Farewell, beautiful Venice ! "

We left Florence yesterday at two o'clock and travelled by an express train until eleven o'clock last night to reach Venice. This morning for the first time I felt like calling a halt; as you remember, I was in Venice last summer. I said to our party, unless I can in some way be a help this morning, I wish you would go without me; for not only was I tired, but I wanted

to be left with my Bible and pen and
paper. So here I am in one of the
grandest hotels I was ever in. Our
private parlor overlooks the Grand
Canal; the golden room is flooded with
golden sunshine, and I am resting as I
could not even on a gondola.

Of course this afternoon I will pay
my respects to St. Mark's and the aris-
tocratic pigeons, etc. I see that by
having this quiet hour I can catch up
the thread that I laid down in Rome.

I was sorry that I could not accept
Mrs. Clark's invitation (wife of the
President of our Theological Seminary
in Rome and daughter of Dr. Butts of
Drew Theological), who kindly offered
to take me to the other side of the Tiber
to see what I could in so short a time
of the work of our Woman's Foreign
Missionary Society. But in returning

Mrs. Clark's call on me, I had to tell
her all our arrangements had been al-
tered, for it had been found out that in
order to be in Switzerland at Interlaken
on Easter, we should have to leave earlier
than we had anticipated, and so I not
only missed going with Mrs. Clark, but
was obliged to go in the afternoon of
the day on which I was to speak on the
work of the King's Daughters in our
American Church.

I was so disappointed, and so were the
Daughters who wear our little silver cross,
but we had to start for Florence. Never
had the words that I had given to my
friends before leaving home been put to
a severer test, —

"'Tis equal joy to go or stay."

It is much easier to theorise than to act;
but I am glad of the line that precedes
the above, —

Venice

"But with a God to guide our way,
'T is equal joy to go or stay."

The joy will come in either going or staying, in recognising our Guide and doing His will. Some one says, "Travel is the fool's paradise." I don't think the fools have a paradise at all. It takes a wise person to have a paradise, whether at home or abroad. I believe the people who travel for mere pleasure do not find it. You come to know of so much unhappiness that people have who are travelling. Sometimes you are compelled to listen to sounds that tell a sad story of domestic life, or domestic death.

During the last moments I spent in my room in the Grand Hotel in Rome, the smile did not leave my face as I listened to a gentleman whistling in the room next to mine. He commenced whistling, —

"I dreamt that I dwelt in marble halls."

A Sunshine Trip

I smiled as I wondered whether he had
awakened from his dream. Just then his
tune changed, and he whistled a tune
called "Dennis" that I always associate
with

"A charge to keep I have,
A God to glorify,
A never-dying soul to save,
And fit it for the sky."

While I was thinking, "Well, if you
really get to that, it will not matter
whether your dream of dwelling in marble halls comes true or not," again the
tune changed, and the song we heard so
often on the trip was beautifully whistled
("The Palms"); and then he started in
on,

"O Beulah Land! Sweet Beulah Land!"

Well, the whole thing was a sermon to
me; and to tell the truth I have to catch
my sermons as best I can on this trip.

So I arranged it all, commencing with

" Dreaming dreams of a life that is not,
Of a life that can never be,"

then awakening to see that life must have a purpose in it, that we have " a charge to keep." Then coming in sight of a cross and seeing a life laid down for us, and this bringing us sooner or later in view of the Delectable Mountains, we finally catch a sight of the New Jerusalem, that will " never pass away."

"O Beulah Land ! Sweet Beulah Land !"

Of course I had prepared myself for the disappointment of staying so short a time in Florence. It could only be a bird's-eye view, seeing a few paintings and pieces of sculpture ; but the old familiar hymn, " Work, for the night is coming," will never be disassociated from Michael Angelo's last piece of work,

"Night and Morning," which I saw in Florence. Are we doing work that will be worth looking at even if unfinished?

The holy Robert McCheyne sealed all his letters with a device of the sun going down behind the western hills, and over it these words, "The night cometh."

W E left Milan at night, and the next morning we were nearing the spot where we had expected to take the train for Interlaken. But we had decided to go right on to Paris. So the sunset on the Jungfrau I should not see. But I had seen it, and it was "within" me. Had I not gazed at the celestial vision, and longed for purity, — had it not made me hungry more than once, to know what the bridal of the soul must be? So I looked at it, as memory brought it before me, as we passed the region of the Alps, and I had a sort of feeling that "what thou hast not now, thou shalt have hereafter." There is much we must learn to wait for, and our lives, I am sure, would be much happier if we would wait in hope. It is only a question of time when we shall have all things. ⸌We are heirs of all things, and we shall come into our inheritance some day. ⸗ There is a deeper meaning and greater joy in " Hope in the Lord " than some of us have ever known.⸜ So I passed the Alps in *hope*.

We reached Paris on the eve of Easter. The beautiful Easter ! I did not grieve that we had missed being in Rome on Easter. It was impossible to be in Jerusalem, where of course we should have been so delighted to be on Easter. Yet we had learned that in our dreams we had not counted on some facts, for we were in Rome on Palm Sunday ; and I noticed we had not the same desire to remain over Easter that we had had. So on Easter Sunday morning in Paris, in the quiet of my room, I saw that the lesson had gone down deeper, — " The Kingdom

(the Easter) is within you." One does
not reach this experience quickly. I was
told when a child that the sun danced on
Easter Sunday morning; so that if it
rained and the new bonnet could not be
worn, I had no Easter. Of course that
was a very early stage, but the later stages
were foolish too; but I knew that Sunday
morning in Paris, that nothing could pre-
vent me from having an Easter, for He
had become my Easter, and as the picture
at the tomb had always taught — it was
her name uttered by the voice of love,
and her glad recognition of her Master
that made the real Easter, for one
woman : so I had my Easter in Paris, but
Paris did not make my Easter. I saw on
that day for the first time the wonderful
Church of the Madeleine lighted with
innumerable candles ; and the finest singing I ever heard in a church I heard that

afternoon. The effect was wonderful, and yet there is a glory that excelleth — the inward glory of the Spirit; for the music ceases; the flowers die on the altar, but the glory of an inward Christ abideth forever. That which will continue longest with me, as associated with my visit to Paris, was a gift I received, which cannot be taken from me. I know it was given to Saint Paul in the first place, but it was surely given to me on the night of Easter day. " My grace is sufficient for thee." It was spoken to my inner consciousness. I said, " Is it sufficient for all my sinful past?" And the answer came — "Sufficient!" I said, "Is it sufficient for all my future?" and the answer came — " Sufficient!" Sufficient " grace to cover all my sins," and sufficient grace with every thorn and for every duty. And it was made very clear to me by the

Spirit that it was *His* grace that was sufficient and *not mine*. I could not depend
on any grace but His grace ; and that was
to be given me just to meet every need.
I was to draw on Him for his grace moment by moment. That was enough,
that was more to me than all the sights
of earth, — *that* met my deepest need, and
that was a preparation for the news which
came the next day, — that enabled me to
resign the determination that the ending
of the trip should find me at Tavistock,
where I should look at the words: "Oh,
bliss of the purified" and "Thou shalt
guide me with thy counsel, and afterwards
receive me to glory," and where I should
read again the words cut in the stone, that
I had heard the voice that is now still
utter so many times, "The Spirit and the
Bride say come." But if dear M——
is so ill as the letter says, then I must

return to see her before she sails for old England; and only a few days remain, so I shall not see the spot so sacred to me. Mrs. Munro is more than willing to change from the " Lucania " to the "Campania" which will sail in a few days. So with only a mere call in London (the city so fascinating to me) we sail on the " Campania " for New York. We have been far from our home. We have passed dangers seen and unseen. We have enjoyed much, — learned much, and we feel sure that while other places may fade or grow dim in our memory, the land of His birth, — the land where He worked and suffered and died, will be an unfading memory with us. Disappointed we may have been in much of the Holy Land or in the absence of what we had expected to see, but after all it was the Holy Land, and it was the Jerusalem that we hoped, with the pious Jews, would yet be the joy of earth ; and the echo of the voices of the angel who stood by the side of the disciples we seemed to hear, as we left the sacred spot: "This same Jesus which is taken up from you unto heaven shall so come in like manner as ye have seen Him go unto heaven." We left Jerusalem with the faith and hope that His feet would again stand on the Mount of Olives.

And yet I keep saying, "Can it be I have been in the Jerusalem where He set His face to go and suffer?" For "He set His face steadfastly towards Jerusalem," and after Him the grand Apostle said, "I go bound in the spirit unto Jerusalem, not knowing the things that shall befall me there, save that bonds and imprisonment await me." Oh, there is a "Jerusalem, the golden," for all those who have suffered in this Jerusalem : —

A Sunshine Trip

"These are they who bore the cross;
Nobly for their master stood;
Sufferers in His righteous cause;
Followers of their dying God."

How slow we are to enter into His sufferings, not seeing that this is the only way to enter into His glory! We need not go to the Holy Land to see the place of His suffering. He is being crucified in New York! The bloody sweat is wherever the cry of the oppressed is heard, for there is still a suffering Christ. Alas, that the church should not see more deeply into the meaning of all their appeals! Those who love Christ will make the land where they have lived and died for ever fragrant with their memories. We must come to the willingness and the joy of being crucified with Christ, or we shall never know the power of His resurrection.

WE have stepped on English soil at last, the soil so precious to me. The ugly channel, as it has been called, was as lovely and smooth as the Hudson; no one thought of being ill. On my way up to London, the wonderful trip nearly over, I went back in thought, as one always does, to the one spot, the Holy Land. I was glad to think that in all the beautiful pictures in our New Testament (and now I know the land as well as the book) none could be lovelier than that one where He stood by a grave; and in that grave was the body of one whom Jesus loved.

And if it be true that all the beautiful words and truths He uttered are only specimens, a little of the ore of the mines of truth and love, only think what fortunes are ahead of us ; for with Him it is always : " As it was in the beginning, is now, and ever shall be."

We have to remain here a few hours for our steamer, and of course we have paid our respects to St. Paul's and beautiful Westminster. We saw them as the sun was setting ; for in London, as everywhere else, the bright sunshine is with us. One is hardly surprised at the absence of sunshine in London ; so we feel especially grateful that we can have even here the memory of its presence.

THE voyage is ended!
I cannot send out this little book
without thanking the many who prayed
for a safe journey and a safe return.
How many prayed that the seas might
be smooth, and their prayers were answered! The Mediterranean will ever
remain in memory the "Smiling Mediterranean." The stormy Atlantic was
not the name for the beautiful Atlantic
we crossed. Did He say in answer to
so many prayers, " Peace, be still "? It
hardly seemed any time after we stepped
on the " Campania," before we were looking for the faces that three months before

we strained our eyes to see as we passed
from the shore, still waving to them when
they were out of our sight. One who
threw me a bunch of violets, who reached
the steamer too late to come on board
(his eager, happy face I see now as I
write), has reached the eternal shore.
With him the storms are all over. Will
he meet me with fadeless flowers when
the sea of life is crossed? I am glad he
threw me the violets. We shall be glad
some day for all the flowers we have
given or received. As I stood on the
" Campania " as she neared the dock, and
the faces of my boys became clear to
me, a strange gentleman standing in
front of me said, as he stepped back,
" Take my place, madam ; there is no one
looking for me." God grant, when the
voyage of life is over, all the seas,
whether calm or smooth, crossed, we may

be able to say, "Almost Home," and not have to add, "There's no one looking for me." We have now the power to make that saying impossible. Love never forgets. If we have helped souls to that further shore, they will come to see us land.